The Long Trail North

The Long Trail North

KELLY P. GAST

DOUBLEDAY & COMPANY, INC.

GARDEN CITY, NEW YORK

1976

ISBN: 0-385-11501-6
Library of Congress Catalog Card Number: 76-2993

The Long Trail North

The sternwheeler skipper smiled thinly. "Way I heard it down in Okanogan, the only choice you got is take it or leave it."

Dave Watkins stared at the low August river. Salmon were still running, but soon the steamers would stop coming. His beef was ready. But in 1897 things just weren't that good for the cattle business. When, he wondered, had they ever been?

First it had been Indians, then rustlers. By the time Dave had grown to manhood, the railroads were in cahoots with the steamboats to grab the cattleman where it hurt. And after all these years he had an Indian problem again. The men who had driven the herd down from the high range looked at Dave, sensing his despair. Dave turned back to the waiting steamboat skipper. "At that price I'll lose everything," he said.

"Mr. Watkins, everybody has problems. I just haul cattle for a living." From his lean, dyspeptic look, Dave suspected the steamboat skipper's problem was his stomach. He sensed his men's eyes on him. They had problems too. Families to feed. "If I let you haul my cattle I'm broke," Dave said. "So I might just as well go broke without troubling you."

The steamboat man shrugged. "You'll change your mind," he said. "Oh, yeah, here's your mail." He tossed a bundle of letters and month-old newspapers.

Dave caught it. He signaled and his men began chivvying the herd back up the forty hoof-riven miles of uphill trail to Conconully, which is pronounced with the accent on the *null*. Behind him he could feel the steamboat skipper's unbelieving eyes. Finally the whistle gave a derisive toot and the *Evalina* backed away from the landing. Dave waited until she was out of sight around the bend, then let his tired horse stand.

The men looked at him. He nodded. Tiredly, they slipped from their horses. The cattle scattered, seeking out the thin August graze of cheat grass. John Whitefeather came close. "Not good?" he asked.

Dave shook his head. He riffled through the envelopes. Mostly they were ads for things the ranch couldn't afford. There was one from the bank in Okanogan that he didn't bother to open. The newspapers were trying to stir up trouble with Spain. There was some mention of a new gold strike in the Klondike, wherever that was. He stuffed the lot into his saddlebag and looked despairingly at the herd. It was too late to start driving them back up to Conconully. They began making camp.

Morning dawned bright and clear, but the old problems were still there. Kevin Corcoran, whose face was broad, flat, and dark, and who had hair like a horse's tail, was struggling to start a fire of gnarled sagebrush. Dave gave him the mail for kindling. Finally the pungent smoke thinned out and they sat round the fire waiting for coffee and biscuits. Dave perused the month-old papers trying to find some hint of good news.

The Indians were as somber as he, which was not like their usually cheerful nature. He knew they were worried too. His Indians were more tied down than he was, for Dave Watkins, if he starved out in Conconully, could always move on. When an Indian couldn't make it in his own country, where did he go—back to the reservation, where the beef ring could slowly starve him to death?

Dave was thinking about the pole corrals and log cabins of the home range when John Whitefeather approached him again. John was older than Dave and had worked for his father. After a turbulent youth the Indian had renounced the devil and his works. Now that he no longer drank, John Whitefeather was a very stable man. "Not good?" he asked.

Dave shook his head. "We're too damn far away. Everybody gets rich except the men who raise the beef." He paused long enough to construct a cigarette. He offered the bag to John, who shook his head. "What we need is to drive the beef to market ourselves."

"Fat chance," John muttered.

He was right, of course. Chicago was thousands of miles east, first downriver by steamer, then several hundred miles of backtracking by rail while travel time gouged the fat from cattle and bank balances. Seattle— It wasn't much of a town, and it was 130 miles southwest over impossible mountains, or 500 winding miles by riverboat, then a 100-mile drive north.

But somehow the idea wouldn't leave Dave alone. It was August already and there hadn't been all that much rain. The hay in the high meadows was scanty. The bears were hungry and had taken to killing calves, which was never a good sign.

He pored through the month-old papers. If he and his Indians were to survive the winter it could only be at the expense of the herd. The Indians sat smoking, talking quietly while he studied maps, did sums on scraps of paper, and muttered to himself. "Not good?" John Whitefeather asked.

"Not good," Dave echoed. "If we try to winter back up in Conconully we're goners."

"So what we gonna do?"

"Go someplace else—someplace where there's men and money and not much beef."

"You wanna go China?" Hodge Twofingers asked with a hint of a smile.

"It'd beat sitting here and freezing to death."

"Where we going?" Dan Sinlahekin was a dark, broad-faced boy of eighteen. He was a cousin of some sort to John Whitefeather, but their relationships tended to be mat-rilineal, and Dave had never quite gotten the straight of them.

Dave pointed at the papers. Each succeeding issue told more unbelievable tales about the gold strike in the Klon-dike. He had finally worked out just where the Klondike River was located. He suspected a winter there might be just as cold as one in Conconully, and Dave had heard enough stories about gold strikes not to believe everything he read. But other suckers believed them. They would all go haring off to the Klondike.

Dave gave a sour laugh. Conconully winters hit forty below. He didn't know much about Alaska, but it was far-ther north. There was a limit to what cattle could stand, and the beasts were never any great shakes at grazing under ten feet of snow. Besides, the fools who chased up North would mostly starve, and those who didn't would return broke and broken.

Then he thought of another possibility. The men who were going to Alaska— Right now he was willing to bet that the coastal ports would be crammed with eager gold seekers, each with an appetite. If he could just get these critters a few hundred miles over to Portland or Seattle . . . He turned to his people. "I can't pay wages any more, but if we make it I'll go shares. Anybody want to go?"

"I'll go," Fred Cheewack said. "Where we goin'?"

The other men were suddenly cheerful.

"We all going?" Cheewack asked.

Dave had been worrying over this. "I think maybe you better stay," he said. "Try to keep a few cows and one bull— maybe old Shakespeare. If we make any money we'll have to start another herd."

Cheewack nodded. It would be difficult to know whether

he was pleased or disappointed. He saddled his pinto and began riding the uphill miles back to Conconully. Nearing the top of the first ridge, he stopped to yell, "How soon you come back?"

Dave hadn't the slightest idea how long it would take to get a herd to the coast. "Maybe spring," he called. Cheewack waved and disappeared over the hump.

"How do we get there?" John Whitefeather asked.

Dave shrugged. "If these teakettle skippers weren't all thieves we could take a boat down to Portland."

"That's a lot of 'if,'" Whitefeather said. He was a thin man, half a head taller than Dave, lean-faced and with a high-bridged nose. He was coppery red and wore his hair in twin braids. "But we got no money, so what do we do?"

"Drive," Dave said. "We can cut across the bend providing we get through before it snows."

"How long you figure to Portland?" Whitefeather insisted.

Dave shrugged. "Maybe a month."

"Damn," the Indian muttered. "We better get movin'."

To drive cattle is to get tired. Most of all, to drive cattle is to eat dust and to raise a thirst that can surpass any dehydration Kipling could discover east of Suez. By evening fourteen sunlit hours had passed and they had hoorahed cattle down the river valley, through the single main street of Okanogan, past the false-fronted building where a banker in pepper-and-salt suit cast an unbelieving eye on their operation.

As soon as he could, the banker stepped across the dust-runneled street to the courthouse. There was a bass-voiced commotion audible even above the bawling of the herd, and a half hour later the sheriff came galloping up behind them, yelling unkind words because he had to eat dust. Finally he was at the head of the herd where Dave rode. "You can't do this," he shrilled.

The sheriff was a beefy-faced man who smelled of cigars and good whiskey and was used to getting his own way. Dave hoorahed a wandering steer back onto the trail and turned to the beefy man. "Can't do what?" he asked.

"You can't take that herd out of the county."

"Why can't I?"

"You owe the bank."

"Ain't ever gonna pay the bank either if I don't sell this beef, now am I?"

The sheriff chewed over this, spurring his horse to keep up with Dave at the head of the herd. "There's a law," he warned.

"There sure is," Dave said. "And you better go back and read up on it. Lawman goes tryin' to restrain trade and do a banker's dirty work foreclosin' on a note before it's due—that poor sheriff just might find himself behind bars, and I'll bet you that banker wouldn't even bring him a file."

The sheriff glowered. "You better not—"

"And besides," Dave continued, "a poor lawman just doin' his duty for a hundred dollars a month shouldn't have to try to stand up against a bunch of wild Indians."

The sheriff glanced nervously behind at the cowboys bringing up the rear of the herd. The dust was too thick for him to tell how many there were. Suddenly there was a war whoop from the rear. Dave recognized Dan Sinlahekin's happy sound. To the lonesome sheriff it must have sounded differently. He glowered at Dave. "You ain't heard the last of this," he promised. As the sheriff rode off at an angle to get around the herd, Dave knew the thin-voiced man was probably telling the truth.

Hours later they camped in a horseshoe bend where the herd could graze on still green grass. Dave got out of his dusty clothes and slipped into the river, which was amazing cold for August. He dressed again and started the fire while the other cowboys bathed, whooping and hollering as they contacted the frigid water. It was an easy camp, with only a couple of hundred yards to patrol on the landward side of the horseshoe. They supped coffee and biscuits and four-day-old beef that was starting to turn. Dave set night watches and rolled up in his saddle blanket.

When he woke, a stranger had joined the camp. He seemed to be a traveling man, with a horse for riding and another for packing. The stranger sat quietly by the fire sharing a bottle of whiskey with Dave's people.

Now that, Dave thought, *is exactly what I don't need!* His people were all good boys and men, but they weren't used to some things. He remembered what a heller John Whitefeather had been before he had seen the light through a glass darkly and changed his ways. And Dan Sinlahekin was only eighteen!

It was a clear, moonlit night without a hint of breeze. Instantly Dave saw that half the herd was already out of the horseshoe, fanning out up the hillside. Which meant whoever was on watch . . . Dave pulled on his boots. After a moment's thought he strapped on his pistol too.

When he reached the dying fire, the stranger was all boozy affability. "Howdy," he said. "Hear you been havin' some trouble." He was a cheerful wanderer in battered derby and a stained twill suit. Even over the odor of cheap whiskey Dave could sense the more pungent aromas of sensen and the four-dollar-a-barrel cigars that had altered the color of the stranger's flowing mustache. Dave wondered.

His people lay about with silly grins, laughing at nothing. Hodge Twofingers held the bottle, his face sweaty as he tilted it. Hodge was a good horseman and one of the best men Dave had ever known with cows. But he had his weakness.

The boys, Kevin Corcoran and Dan Sinlahekin, were staring with unfocused eyes into the dying fire. But what horrified Dave most was John Whitefeather. The older man was laughing and smiling too, very unlike his usual God-fearing self. And the cattle were spreading farther uphill.

For an instant Dave felt murderous rage. The stupid SOB was only trying to be friendly, but he was giving booze to Indians and minors. What would happen if Dave were suddenly to break up the fun? His people were good people, but they had only been civilized for half a century. Unlike whites, they did not have a four-thousand-year-old past that had weeded out those least able to withstand the ravages of booze.

"Sit down, podner, have a little snort of the cup that cheers."

Dave had to get rid of this menace before the herd was totally scattered. "You're breaking several laws," he said.

"Law? Ain't no law in this country!"

Despite the bank's hip-pocket sheriff up in Okanogan, Dave knew the stranger was close to the truth. "I'm sorry," he said, "but you'll have to put it away."

"Awww, come on, now!"

Abruptly Dave knew the affable stranger was neither drunk nor affable. And just as abruptly he knew this was how the sheriff of Okanogan county was going to keep his herd from paying off any loan. He turned to John Whitefeather. "I thought you were a God-fearing man!"

Whitefeather gave a solemn wink. Dave wondered how much the older Indian had drunk. The young men would be useless for hours. And the cattle were scattering.

"I'll have a drink," Dave said suddenly. He took the bottle and tilted it, blowing into the bottle and creating bubbles. In the process he got a taste of what was undoubtedly the vilest whiskey in the Northwest. "Now you." He handed the bottle back to the stranger.

The stranger faked a swallow.

"Not that way," Dave said.

The stranger was suddenly not drunk at all.

"Drink," Dave said. The Indians were all looking at the stranger.

Unwillingly, the stranger swallowed.

"You've got some catching up to do," Dave said. "Have another." He turned to his Indians. "Your friend here hasn't been hitting it as hard as you," he explained. "Maybe he needs drenching."

The boys giggled, and suddenly it was all a big happy game. They raided the stranger's pack and found another full bottle. They teased it open, and Kevin handed it to the gasping stranger, who had just swallowed a quarter pint, finishing the last bottle. When the stranger hesitated, Twofingers and Taskoosh caught his arms and tilted his head back.

Basically, it was like drenching a horse with a pound of salts. But in this case they drenched the affable stranger with a quart of his own whiskey.

2

Gasping and swearing, the stranger staggered to his feet. He said unkind things about Dave and about Indians in general, but within something under a minute his enunciation deteriorated. Soon he sat with his head between his knees.

Dave inspected the man's gear. He had packed no provisions for travel apart from a single blanket. No groceries— nothing except whiskey. Dave knew now that his suspicions had been correct. He turned to see John Whitefeather observing him. "I thought you didn't drink any more."

"I don't," Whitefeather said with a faint grin. "Who you think chunked horseturds until you woke up?"

"Oh!" They faced each other in the moonlight.

"What you want to do with the banker's friend?"

"Scalp him," Dave said. "But I know who'd get blamed."

"Yes," Whitefeather said soberly. "We can't have him dying on us."

They returned to the lethargic stranger, who by now lay face down. John Whitefeather put his finger down the man's throat until he vomited a gushing stream of redolent liquid. Finally they had the man on his way, feet tied together beneath his horse's belly and his horse aimed toward Okanogan with a slap on the rump. Whitefeather gazed at the other cowboys, shaking his head. The boys were both asleep. Twofingers and Taskoosh were wobbly, but under

John's urging they managed to sit their horses. The four of them chased off up the hillside and began encouraging the straying cattle back into the horseshoe bend.

Finally the herd was bedded down. Dave let the Indians go to sleep while he stood watch. He wondered what the bank and its hip-pocket sheriff would try next. Somewhere over the ridge of the hill a coyote howled at the moon. He checked the load in his octagonal-barreled .45-.90. Soon he was going to have to buy ammunition.

Sleepily, he patrolled the open end of the horseshoe, chivvying the couple of dozen steers who refused to stop trying to escape up the hill again. On three sides the river gurgled, glistening in the moonlight like some gigantic snake. Dave considered the river. Twenty miles south of here it flowed into the Columbia. They could follow the big river to Portland, but it was a five-hundred-mile circle through scant cheat grass range that would not support a cow on five acres. And somewhere along the way he was sure to run into homesteaders who would not take kindly to a herd being driven through. And there were Indians, not all of them as decent and hard-working as his friends.

The first real town would be Wenatchee, some eighty-five miles south of here. There, unless the bank and its hip-pocket sheriff had roused the whole country against him by then, he could sell a beef or two for salt, cartridges, and enough flour to last them through the mountains. His reverie was interrupted by a distant coughing sound.

At first he thought it was some kind of a nightbird, then unbelieving, he realized what the sound really was. That steady chuff-chuff could only be the exhaust of a steam engine. He wondered for an instant if the skipper who had delivered his mail was coming back up to offer better terms. But the water in August was too low for second thoughts.

Then abruptly Dave knew the only thing that could make the teakettle skipper hang around here. The bank owned him too. That affable traveling man with no baggage except whiskey had not planned on spending a night alone in the wilds. Aboard the steamer would be a crew of ruffians ready to load cattle. They would be counting on the whiskey peddler to have the Indians out of action. And Dave? Soberly he realized the affable stranger had probably planned something else for him. He spurred his horse over to where the Indians slept.

John Whitefeather had already heard the sound. He was pulling on his boots. They looked at each other in the bright moonlight, and Dave realized the older man had guessed what was coming too. Dave thought a moment. The bank had gone beyond the law this time. They knew it, and their hip-pocket sheriff must know it too. Whatever they planned would of necessity demand that there be no survivors to complain to an impartial court—if such a thing could be found anywhere in this sparsely settled country.

Dan and Kevin moaned but were too full of booze to awaken properly. It didn't make that much difference, Dave guessed. They didn't have enough rifles to go around. Twofingers had an ancient single-shot piece. John Whitefeather had nothing. Dave had his pistol and his .45-.90. He held them up, wondering which the older Indian would take. John hesitated a moment, then took the pistol. "Can't hit anything with it," John said ruefully, "but neither can you. At least I know *you* can hit something with the rifle."

The steamboat's chuffing was louder, but the boat was still out of sight. Echoes rebounded from the sides of the valley which, at this point, was something over a mile across with nearly vertical five-hundred-foot walls up to the next flat. It had not been the smartest thing he had ever done, Dave guessed, to bed down in this horseshoe bend. There was a gently sloping riverbank on three sides. They could be loading cattle aboard the steamer within minutes. How many men, he wondered?

A horse snorted on the hill behind him. Dave whirled with his rifle at the ready. The moonlight made everything light as day, yet for a moment he could not see the other rider. Then he saw the horse with a man stretched low over its neck. He nearly fired before he realized what it was. The affable, whiskey-dispensing stranger was still lolling unconscious atop his mount. The horse, lacking further instructions, had returned to seek out the companionship of its own kind among their mounts. Dave had nearly shot the drunken stranger!

John Whitefeather was urging the others into hiding around the curve of the horseshoe. Still the steamboat did not appear. Dave struggled to control his mounting tension. Only one day on the trail and already he was starting to come apart. How was he ever going to make it to the coast?

Suddenly he realized the jig would be up if they saw the stranger tied to his horse. He galloped uphill and whacked the beast over the rump with a lariat end until it turned and trotted back toward Okanogan. This was never going to work. There would be a dozen men aboard the sternwheeler. Then he saw the only way it could be made to work. He spurred his horse around the edge of the horseshoe, splashing through the shallows until he caught up with Whitefeather. "Unsaddle," he said. "Let them see your horse without a man on it. And bring everybody back to camp quick before they come in sight."

John Whitefeather was plainly mystified. But he did as told. Dave galloped back to camp and unsaddled. He ignored the restless steers who were preparing to bolt uphill again. He poured water over the boys, but they only coughed and groaned. He prayed nothing would happen to them.

The moon was high—too high, the night too bright. He got Whitefeather, Twofingers, and Taskoosh together. Twofingers and Taskoosh were taciturn, competent men in their early thirties. During the boom year when it had looked as if Conconully might turn into a real town, Dave and Taskoosh had attended school together.

Dave stared at the river. The echoes off the mile-wide valley walls were confusing, but he knew the steamer would heave into view any minute now. The horseshoe bend was nearly treeless, actually nothing but a grassed-over sandspit that would be under water half the year. But one corner held a clump of waterlogged poplars. They hurried toward the shelter of the trees and settled down to wait. "What we gonna do?" Twofingers asked.

"They want to load our cattle aboard that steamboat," Dave said. "There'll be more of them than us, so maybe we better let them."

Twofingers gave him an odd look. Just then the sternwheeler rounded the bend, moving cautiously downriver. There was a change in the sound of the engines, and a moment later Dave realized she was backing. The sternwheeler was moving oddly, as if the pilot was unsure of the current. She skidded up onto the bank farther than Dave would have thought necessary. There was the sound of the Lord's name being taken in vain several times as the huge sternwheel began backing again. "Rock it, you fatheads, or we'll be here all winter," an angry, bullroaring voice called. Dave was sure he recognized that basso voice.

He waited in the poplars, watching with the three Indians still able to navigate while the steamboaters—there seemed to be quite a few of them—congregated at one rail. They began charging en masse back and forth across the deck, trying to rock the boat loose while the sternwheel struggled to throw more water up under the grounded bow. To everyone's surprise their efforts were successful. The sternwheeler groaned off the grassy bank and floated level again. This time the pilot nosed ashore with less enthusiasm.

The gangway dropped from the bow and men scrambled ashore, pulling a prefabricated fence of rope and poles, which they began setting up in a huge V with the small end to the gangway. A dozen men began hoorahing cattle aboard the steamer.

Whitefeather looked at Dave. "Too many," he muttered. "They kill us."

Dave shrugged. "We'll starve anyway. What're Indians supposed to be good at?"

Taskoosh and Twofingers grinned. Holding their single weapon high, they stepped out of the poplars into waist-deep water. The moon was still high and Dave was sure they would be seen, but the men ashore were too busy loading cattle to bother with odd-shaped bits of debris that floated toward the steamboat. Dave and Whitefeather followed, holding their guns out of the water. To Dave's surprise there was a back current along the bank that would have made their drift logical if anyone had paid attention. At any rate, it made it easier to wade chest deep in the chill water.

They caught the rub rail along the edge of the flat-bottomed hull and began pulling themselves sternward. There was still bottom beneath their feet, but Dave knew any minute a pothole would come along to complicate things. Then his hands encountered a projection. They were in shadow now, and the bright-as-day moon no longer co-operated. He discovered a ladder built into the lowest spot amidships. He gripped his .45-.90 with his left hand and began climbing.

The deck was only three feet above water level at this point. But it was already filling with spooky cattle who could recognize a man on horseback, but were not willing to accord the same respect to a man on foot. Thirty feet away was a stairway up to the pilothouse and cabin deck. Dave vaulted over the rail. There was nobody down here with the cattle. Amidships he caught the eerie glow of flames from an open firebox, but there was no one in sight. The men on shore had their hands full trying to crowd more cattle aboard. Waving his hat and slapping the faces of horn-happy steers, Dave bobbed and weaved his way to the stairway. Moments later the three Indians crouched there with him.

They checked their weapons. Dave began creeping up the stairway. Below him cattle bawled, hooves drumming on the splintery deck. He wondered why he was being so quiet. At the head of the stairway moonlight showed. He poked a cautious head through the opening. Nobody in sight.

There had to be somebody below firing boilers, he guessed. But with cattle stomping and bawling, the black gang would be isolated in their miniature hell. Taskoosh and Twofingers began trying the doors of cabins. A couple were locked, but most were open and empty. With Whitefeather watching his back, Dave began moving toward the pilothouse, doing his best to stay in the inky shadows.

There was a change in the sound of the *Evalina*'s engine, and after an instant Dave realized the pilot was backing away. Fifty feet out in the river the steamer halted its backward drift and nudged gently inshore again. The pilot was making sure the added weight of cattle would not leave him stranded on the sandspit. Abruptly Dave realized he might best leave the pilot alone until all the cattle were loaded and they were under way.

He crept along the shadowed side of the upper deck looking for signs of life. There had to be at least one man, probably two down with engines and boilers; and the skipper at the wheel. All the rest were ashore. He reached the bulk of the pilothouse and saw the faint glow of a binnacle lamp. A man stood at the man-high wheel, cranking it back and forth as he struggled to hold the boat on the beach. The paddlewheel was turning very slowly, just enough to give some direction to the rudders.

Then as Dave grew emboldened to raise his head higher, he saw there was a second man in the pilothouse. Dave nearly missed him, for the second man sat in the rear, in the dark, betraying his presence only by the glowing tip of a cigar and a glint of metal in his lap. Dave strained his eyes. He wasn't sure, but it looked like a nickel-plated pistol. A hand touched his shoulder.

Dave struggled not to yell. He ducked below the bottom of the window and saw it was Whitefeather. The older man put his finger to his lips and beckoned.

Dave pointed at the pilothouse. Whitefeather shook his head and beckoned again. Unwillingly, Dave crept along the side deck behind him. Twofingers had jimmied the lock on one of the two cabins they had been unable to enter. He pointed. Dave strained his eyes into the dark hole of the doorway. He could see nothing. After an indecisive moment, Twofingers took his arm and drew him into the cabin.

The engine-room telegraph jangled again, and the paddlewheel began splashing water in the opposite direction. Dave rushed from the darkened cabin and crept as far forward as he dared along the dark side of the deck. The *Evalina* began turning, and he realized that in a moment he would be in bright moonlight. Could they be loaded already? Then he saw that the horseshoe bend was still well populated with milling, bawling cattle. Most of the men were still ashore.

Whoever was piloting either was not very expert or this was a particularly tricky piece of river. The steamer backed nearly to the opposite bank, then made a half circle upstream. As the moonlight crept toward him, Dave flattened himself and prayed that the men in the pilothouse would be too busy to look down.

The man at the wheel said unprintable things about people who could not properly respond to engine-room telegraphs. The instrument jangled again, and the paddlewheel once more reversed direction. The steamboat edged inshore with a slight bump. It was not in exactly the same position as the first time, and the men ashore had to move the wings of their portable rope-and-pole loading fence. Whitefeather was pulling Dave's sleeve again.

Dave followed him back to the cabin, whose door was now shut. Whitefeather tapped on it, then entered, pulling Dave with him. The cabin was in total darkness. Then abruptly there was light and a strong stink of singed hair which, after an instant, Dave realized was from Twofingers' hat, which he had been holding over a tiny lamp. On the lower bunk in the cabin lay a bound and gagged man. Dave stared at him, and after a moment decided he was not seeing things. It was the lean, dyspeptic skipper of the *Evalina!*

3

Dave stared. This was the man who had cheerfully volunteered to ruin him. The tiny cabin was sweltering, and the stink from Twofingers' singed hat was not improving the situation.

Taskoosh was still prowling about outside somewhere.

The dyspeptic sternwheeler skipper glared at the three of them. Dave thought a moment, then pulled the rag from the lean man's mouth. With his finger to his lips, Dave whispered, "What's goin' on?"

"Cut me loose, damn it!"

Dave did. The lean man sat up and rubbed his wrists. "You SOBs'll pay for this!" he snapped.

"If there's any paying, we'll see what's legal about my cattle aboard your boat and no bill of lading. I think the technical word for it is rustling."

Abruptly the lean man became aware of the bawling, stamping cattle below. "What's going on?" he asked.

Dave glared at him. "A while ago you and the bank seemed to know everything."

The captain stopped rubbing his wrists and looked up at Dave. Abruptly his anger left him. "The bank," he muttered, and seemed to shrink into himself. "Them yours?" he asked, pointing at the cattle noises that rose from below.

Dave nodded. "My cattle. But not my men stealing them."

The steamboat skipper pointed at the ropes that had bound him. "It wasn't my idea," he said.

"So where do you stand now?"

"Where do you expect me to stand?" the lean man snapped. "You stand to lose your cattle. I stand to lose my boat!"

"You got a gun?"

"Had one. I s'pose it's gone now. This ain't my cabin."

Somebody knocked on the door. Hastily Twofingers put his hat over the lamp. They opened the door a crack. It was Taskoosh. "They're just about loaded," he warned.

Everybody looked expectantly at Dave. He fingered his .45-.90, wondering what to do next. There ought to be a way to handle this without bloodshed if he could just figure out how. He stepped out of the cabin. The door closed momentarily while Twofingers put out the lamp and rescued his smoking hat, then the others filed down the shady side of the deck toward the pilothouse.

The horseshoe bend was nearly empty of cattle. Loaders were shagging the horses aboard too. One man was already beginning to take down the wings of their loading pen. Dave peered into the pilothouse, where a man wrestled with the man-high wheel. The other still sat in the shadows, nickel-plated pistol glistening in the light of his cigar.

Taskoosh walked around to the other side of the pilothouse and tapped on the glass. The man at the wheel ignored him. The man in the shadows left his chair and, pistol in hand, strolled toward the door. Then Taskoosh turned slightly, and the moonlight silhouetted twin braids. The man inside raised his nickel-plated pistol. Without stopping to think it over, Dave pulled the trigger of his .45-.90.

Flame shot a foot from the muzzle as the pilothouse window shattered. The pistol popped in feeble echo to the boom of Dave's heavy-caliber rifle. Taskoosh dropped. The pistol clattered to the deck in the same instant that the stranger's head abruptly changed shape.

The man at the wheel was turning in horrified surprise as Dave tore through the cabin and out the other door. But when he got there Taskoosh was already getting to his feet. "God damn!," Taskoosh grumbled, "that shypoke shoot at anything."

"Never again, he won't," Dave said. He went back into the cabin. The dyspeptic skipper had wrested the wheel from the pilot's nerveless grasp and was holding the *Evalina* steady against the shore.

So now their surprise was spoiled. The men ashore had to have heard the shot. Dave peered from the open front window of the pilothouse and was abruptly seized with desperate inspiration. "Hurry up and get all that gear and saddles aboard!" he yelled. "We don't want any traces."

Obediently, the men began scouring the horseshoe sandspit, gathering up everything. Whitefeather came up behind Dave. "The boys," he muttered.

Oh, Jesus! Dave had completely forgotten about Dan and Kevin. Then the inspiration of desperation seized him again. The steady chuff of the sternwheeler's engine seemed to be covering up any strangeness in his voice. "You'll find a couple of drunk Indians out there somewhere," he yelled. "Bring them aboard too. And don't hurt them!" he added, "we got enough trouble now."

While three of the men lugged saddles and other equipment onto the gangplank, the others began scouring the sage at the open end of the horseshoe, looking for the drunk Indians. "Ain't nobody here," one yelled after a moment.

"Keep looking. We've got to find them." Turning to the dyspeptic steamboat skipper whose face was grayer than usual as he looked at the body on the pilothouse deck, Dave asked, "Are they armed?"

The lean man swallowed and nodded. "Who's he?" he asked with a gesture at the man Dave had shot.

"Don't you know?"

The skipper pulled the lamp from the binnacle and

brought it down close. The dead man wore a blue serge suit
and a striped shirt without collar. In the corner of the
pilothouse a derby rolled gently back and forth in time with
the pulsations of the steamer's idling wheel. He had been of
average height, sandy-haired, and with two-day-old red
whiskers. One side of his head was missing and the rest so
pulled out of shape by Dave's heavy, low-speed slug that it
was difficult to imagine what he would have looked like
alive.

Whitefeather edged close to Dave. "Boys must've woke
up," he murmured. "Those men out there've walked across
camp two or three times already."

Dave wondered what Kevin and Dan would have done.
Probably, waking up in the midst of the brouhaha of a
dozen strangers driving cattle aboard the *Evalina*, they
would assume the others were scattered or dead. And after
yesterday they would know better than to call on the sheriff
in Okanogan.

He sighed. They could walk the ridge behind Okanogan
and make it back to Conconully with three days of hungry
foot-slogging. Once home Fred Cheewack would take care
of them. But what would Fred do once he got the news that
Dave and his friends were gone, the herd stolen? Dave
wished the boys were here. He was going to need their help.
The strangers were drifting back toward the *Evalina*'s gangplank again.

"Back up the hillside," Dave yelled. "You've got to find
them unless you want to hang." The men made angry ges-
tures in the moonlight, but they wheeled and began comb-
ing the ground away from the steamer again. When they
were a comfortable distance away Dave turned to the lean,
dyspeptic skipper. "Let's go," he said.

The lean man jerked on the telegraph, and bells jangled
below. The chuffing became louder, faster, and the
paddlewheel began dredging out the bottom beneath the
flat-bottomed hull. Then suddenly they were backing. He

jangled the telegraph again and the *Evalina* was heading downstream, already halfway around the horseshoe bend. With the boat's speed augmented by the current, she was moving three times as fast as the waving, cursing men who sprinted across the neck of the bend. The skipper gave them a farewell toot of the *Evalina*'s shrill whistle.

Twofingers was bending over the man who had tried to shoot him. He had appropriated the nickel-plated pistol. Dave guessed he was entitled to it. "Anybody know him?" Dave asked. They shook their heads.

There was a hollow whistle. The man who had been piloting flipped up a hinged lid and yelled "Yeah?" down a speaking tube. There were angry yammerings from below.

"Goldang it, Abe, you think *you* got troubles! Just keep 'er moving another hour and then we can tie up for the night, I guess." The pilot wiped his face and turned to Dave. "Didn't even know what happened," he explained.

"How many men you got down there?"

"Fireman and an engineer."

Dave looked at his people. "Any of you think you could fire a boiler for a few hours?" he asked.

The Indians were badly hung over, but they were also afflicted with guilty consciences. They nodded. But the pilot shook his head. "Wood," he explained. "We were s'posed to load in Okanogan but we hadn't started when all that mob came stormin' aboard."

And they would have done it in such a way that nobody could actually connect the bank with their piratical maneuverings. Dave wondered who the dead man was. The others —it would have been easy enough to scrape them up out of the nearest bar. But now that he had planted the seed about hanging for murder, maybe they would disappear just as quietly back into that bar, for he supposed the men ashore would assume that shot had killed the skipper or pilot.

But what about the boys? Kevin and Dan would be skulking around out there somewhere. There was another whistle.

Pilot and engineer wrangled over the speaking tube. Then the lean skipper took over. He turned to Dave and spread his hands. "Much longer and we'll be dead in midstream."

"What?"

"No steerageway," the lean man explained. "Without a head of steam I got no control over this scow."

"How far are we from where we left them?"

The skipper shrugged. "Maybe ten miles by river. But it makes a bend here. It's only half that overland."

"What about fuel?"

The skipper waved at the low-lying bank. "Danged green poplar won't put out any heat but it might get us to Brewster, providing we got enough dry wood to make it burn at all." He was jangling the telegraph again. The pilot began spinning the man-high wheel. Moments later the *Evalina* bumped gently against the bank. The skipper started to give orders, then realized Dave's Indians might not understand what to do. He sprang from the pilothouse and ran to lower the gangway. While the pilot kept the sternwheeler nuzzling the bank, he splashed ashore and tied up to a likely tree. The man at the wheel signaled "finished with engines." There was a dying wheeze, and the paddle-wheel stopped turning.

Within minutes Dave and his remaining three companions were ashore with axes. While they hastened to fell as many trees as possible, the skipper and his pilot struggled to string ropes through the crowded cattle deck. The poplars were only six to eight inches through, and a half-dozen good swings of an ax sent them toppling. Dave had seen steamboat wood often enough—year-old fir split and stacked neatly in four-foot lengths. He was limbing the first tree when the skipper came ashore trailing a length of rope. He fitted a choker around the butt of the tree and whistled. Steam hissed aboard the sternwheeler and a winch began dragging the whole tree down the deck through bawling cattle.

Four hours later the moon went down. Dave was afraid he would cut a foot off swinging an ax in the dark. Before disaster could strike, the skipper yelled, "That's enough." They went back onto the bottom deck where cattle watched them limb and buck green wood by the light of kerosene lamps. "This stuff gonna burn?" Whitefeather asked.

Dave didn't know. Neither, apparently, did the engineer or fireman, who seemed a new edition of the older man. They carried away leafy branches and stuffed the firebox. Dense white smoke poured from the stack, rising straight into the dawning calm for a couple of hundred yards before the cloud flattened out in a mushroom shape.

It would be visible for miles. Dave wondered if the men who had shagged his cattle aboard were heading back for Okanogan or if they were heading this way to even the score. He was ready to drop from exhaustion, and he knew it would be best to tie up for a while until everyone was rested. But with the kind of law the bank and sheriff were enforcing in Okanogan County it might be wisest to keep moving.

He faced other problems if the hip-pocket sheriff caught him, for between the sheriff and the bank they would some-how manage to turn his killing of the unknown red-whiskered man into murder.

There was an abrupt "whump," and smoke boiled from the firebox, permeating the lower deck with the acrid smell of wet, burning poplar. Then Dave realized what had happened. The firebox full of banked coals had finally dried the charge of leaves and twigs the fireman had stuffed into it. The tall stack was not emitting smoke now. It was shooting sparks like a Roman candle.

The skipper sprang over the gangplank to untie. Abruptly he gave a startled yell. Dave heard a rippling, two-toned war whoop that he recognized as Dan Sinlahekin's happy sound. He ran to the head of the gangplank and yelled,

"Dan, Kevin, turn him loose and come aboard quick. We're leaving!"

Moments later the boys were aboard the *Evalina*, escorting the lean, dyspeptic skipper, who was making noises like a brood hen who has been forced to swim.

Whitefeather and Twofingers were suddenly happy again. They overwhelmed the boys with questions, and Dave wondered how Indians could ever have acquired the label of being a stoic, unemotional people. So now he had five men again. And all he had to do was ride this boat five hundred miles down the winding river to Portland.

He wondered about galley facilities aboard the *Evalina*. So far he had not seen any signs of a cook. But mostly, he wondered if he dared find an empty cabin and sleep for a few hours.

The *Evalina*'s stack was emitting a steady Roman candle eruption of sparks from the green poplar, but the wood seemed to be burning. He supposed the fireman had a small supply of dry fir to encourage the blaze, but now that the engine was running the forced draft would be sufficient to make just about anything burn. How many miles to the next woodpile? He guessed they were halfway from Okanogan to Brewster. The pair of houses that some optimist called Brewster was near the old abandoned Fort Okanogan—where this river flowed into the Columbia. There ought to be wood there. Maybe a sheriff's posse too.

Something was digging at the back of his mind. Then abruptly Dave realized what it was. He had the boys back. Whitefeather and Twofingers had given them joyous greeting. But when was the last time he had seen Arnold Taskoosh? He tried to relax. Taskoosh was tired, asleep in one of the cabins.

But the thought would not let him alone. Tiredly, Dave knew he would not sleep until he was sure his old schoolmate was safe aboard the *Evalina*. He began walking around the cabin deck trying doors. The boys were asleep in one cabin. Two doors down he found Whitefeather and Twofingers pulling off their boots.

The next cabin was empty. The one after that was locked. He passed around the after part of the deck, batting at sparks that threatened to destroy his shirt. The cabins on the other side were all open and empty. He wondered if Taskoosh had somehow been left behind. He wouldn't have gone below to sleep with milling cattle. He had to be in one of these cabins.

When they had first boarded the *Evalina* there had been two locked cabins. The gagged and bound skipper had been aggravating his ulcers in one. The other must be the one that was still locked.

Dave grasped his .45-.90 and trotted back through the shower of sparks on the afterdeck. He tried the door handle again. The cabin was locked. He got out his jackknife and began worrying away at the bolt, which was clearly visible in the gap between the sun-shrunken door and its frame.

There would be a key somewhere. Why was he wasting time this way? Then abruptly the door opened. Taskoosh was inside the cabin. He was stretched out comfortably on a lower bunk, arms behind his head. Across from him in a kitchen chair sat a young woman. She held a small pistol in her hand, pointing it straight at the Indian.

4

Arnold Taskoosh gave Dave an apologetic grin. With a sidelong glance at the girl, he solemnly said, "Ugh."

Dave stared. The girl stared back, unable to decide whether she wanted to point the pistol at Dave or at the Indian. It was a .41 derringer and would make a respectable noise if she pulled that unguarded trigger in this small cabin. And though there was no second shot to worry about, Dave was intensely aware of the damage that first round could do to whoever was in front of it—even if firing it were to break the girl's wrist.

He supposed he ought to be frightened. But piled on top of all the other troubles he'd been having, it was just too much. He gave an inarticulate, full-throated roar like a bear battling bees. The curtain at the cabin's tiny window fluttered. The girl fluttered too as the pistol dropped from her nerveless hand.

Arnold Taskoosh scooped it up before that unguarded trigger could hit the deck. "Ugh," he repeated. "Heap bad medicine."

"Now what happened?" Dave asked.

"Search me," Taskoosh said. "I don't think she speaks much English. Been gruntin' and wavin' guns like this was the Wild West or somethin'."

A moment ago the girl had been pale. Now her face was crimson. "There's nothing wrong with my English!" she snapped. From the sound of it Dave guessed she was from Boston. He tried to conceal his amusement. "If you're going to travel in these parts you'll have to get used to that aboriginal sense of humor," he explained. "And out here it ain't considered polite to point guns even if you do know how to use them."

"But he just came tearing in here like—like some—"

"Yup. And that brings us to another question. There ain't s'posed to be any passengers on this boat so—since you're not from our bunch—" He left it dangling.

"I am most assuredly not from your uh—bunch!" she snapped.

"So if you don't belong to the captain that only leaves the pirates."

"Pirates!" Abruptly the girl came up out of the chair.

"Down!" Dave roared. "Now, who are you and what are you doing here?"

"My name is Emily Jennings. I am from Providence, Rhode Island, and I am returning there with such dispatch as may be possible in this barbarous country."

"Kind of young t'be travelin' alone, ain't you?"

"No, I *ain't*," she said pointedly. "I'm free, white, and twenty-four."

Dave shot Taskoosh a quick glance and raised an eyebrow on his off side. Silently, the Indian oozed from the bunk and out the door. Turning back to the girl, Dave asked, "How far downriver have you booked passage?"

The girl gave a sigh of relief and relaxed slightly. "That awful man!" she said. "He didn't once let on that he could speak English."

"Did you ever try talkin' plain English to him?"

The girl flushed again.

"Mr. Taskoosh is an old and valued friend," Dave said primly. He realized he was bearing down hard on the girl, but it had been a long, sleepless night after a hard day and he'd had enough troubles without some tenderfoot girl pointing a gun at him.

The girl realized abruptly that she had been getting more sympathy out of Taskoosh than she was likely to get from this abrasive white man. She tried to smile. She was, Dave realized, an amazingly attractive young lady so long as she did not have a pistol pointed at anyone. Her hair was done up tight in the style of the nineties, piled high on her head in a blond chignon.

She wore a tweed traveling suit which, though it revealed only her head, her hands, and the toes of her boots, did not seem to be concealing any gross deviations from the female norm. It bulged interestingly in the usual places, and for a moment Dave had trouble concentrating on what he was going to say next. Finally he remembered. "You didn't say how far downriver you've booked passage."

"No, I didn't." Obviously, Miss Jennings was not going to say anything else. The tiny cabin was stifling. He wondered how she kept from melting in that tweed traveling suit, but it was not a fit subject for mixed conversation, so they remained silent. She still sat in the kitchen chair. Dave unlatched the door and put it on the hook and a breeze began flowing through the sweltering cubicle. They studied each other covertly.

"Did you say pirates?" the girl finally asked.

"Good a name as any," Dave said. "They came on this boat and they stole my cattle."

"On this boat?" the girl's eyes grew suddenly round.

Finally Taskoosh was reaching through the gap and getting the door off the hook. He gave Miss Emily Jennings a mournful look and shook his head. "Captain's never heard of her," he said. "No passengers on this run."

Dave studied the girl. "All right," he snapped, "what are their names? How many of them? Who's behind it all? And what's your real name?"

"Emily Jen—uh, Jenkins," she stammered. "But I don't know any pirates."

"Then what are you doing in this den of thieves?"

She bit her lip. "I was, uh— I was engaged for a position that did not fulfill my expectations."

Dave wrinkled his brow. "You mean you quit your job?"

"Well—"

"What you mean is you quit your job and you're on the run. What're you running from?"

"I was engaged as a governess for two motherless children. I assumed the gentleman who engaged me was a widower. Only after a week in his house did I learn that his wife left him for excellent reasons. Under the circumstances I could hardly stay."

Dave supposed she could not.

The *Evalina*'s paddlewheel changed its rhythm. He stepped out of the cabin and saw it was starting to dawn. The *Evalina* still spouted twin Roman candles of sparks from side-by-side stacks, but the boat was slowing. He got around the cabins to the starboard side and saw the two or three houses and rickety dock that were Brewster. More importantly, he saw the pile of seasoned firewood stacked in four-foot lengths at the head of the dock. A bell jingled below him, and a moment later the *Evalina* shuddered as the paddlewheel began backing.

So they had reached the fork where the Okanogan pours into the Columbia. He was still only twenty miles from where the pirates had loaded his cattle. The river was so low that even if the *Evalina* had had properly seasoned firewood she couldn't have moved any faster. He wondered where the pirates were now. And that hip-pocket sheriff? Were they working together? Didn't stand to reason that there'd be two separate sets of rustlers after his herd in a single day.

The steamer bumped gently into the dock, and men jumped off with lines. Within minutes the lean dyspeptic skipper had organized his engineer and fireman along with all of Dave's Indians he could collar and they were lugging firewood, piling it on the front apron within inches of the bawling cattle. Dave studied the herd. How long before he would have to feed and water them? How long before trouble came riding over the hill from Okanogan way? It was no time for maundering. He left the girl in the cabin and went below to help load wood.

A four-foot stick of seasoned fir is not exactly a fence post. But trotting the length of the dock and onto the foredeck of the *Evalina* with an armload of fir, Dave discovered after the fourth trip, could be almost as bone-wearying as breaking horses. It was broad daylight by now, though the sun had not yet risen. August in this latitude meant it was about four o'clock. Already there was a hint of the enervating sun and heat that would last for sixteen searing, uninterrupted hours. If they could just get enough wood on board to give the *Evalina* steerageway for the next seventy miles to Wenatchee . . .

Maybe he could get some rest. Trotting the length of the dock with his fifth armload of wood, Dave realized dully that it had been somewhere between three and five days since he'd gotten a full night's sleep. And with this heat he'd have to rig watering troughs and scoop buckets up from the river unless the overworked engineer had some way to pump water up for his cattle to drink.

Dan Sinlahekin and Kevin Corcoran seemed to have recovered from the affable stranger's bad whiskey, which reminded Dave to wonder if the stranger had. Or was his horse still wandering somewhere south of Okanogan? It would be wisest, he supposed, never to get within range of that affable stranger if he ever happened to have a gun in his hands. The boys were shouting and war whooping as they lugged firewood. Was I like that when I was eighteen, Dave wondered? He was sweating profusely, but they had to get this wood loaded and be on their way before . . .

John Whitefeather was passing him empty-handed, heading ashore for another load when abruptly the older man said, "Oh, oh! Here they come."

The *Evalina's* whistle shrilled at that same instant, and suddenly firewood was forgotten in the frantic scramble to cast off lines and get aboard before the horsemen could come pounding down the hill and— Staring from the foredeck of the backing steamer, Dave realized there must be twenty of them. There was a zinging hiss, and an instant later he heard the crack of a rifle.

He rushed to the upper deck and found his octagonal-barreled .45-.90. He didn't expect to hit anything at this distance, but when it boomed the horsemen scattered in sudden consternation, and their downhill charge was abruptly something less than pell mell.

Jesus, he thought. What's happening to the law in this country? He wondered if this was the banker's and the sheriff's doing. Was it a legal posse chasing him like some criminal? Or was this some other lot of ruffians in business for themselves? The *Evalina* tooted her whistle. The engineroom telegraph jangled, and once more they were moving downstream, hugging the opposite bank from the band of horsemen.

Suddenly he remembered the girl. She must be terrified. The poor girl had come from the East, from settled country. She'd been suckered into some dirty old man's house, and when she tried to escape she had ended up in the midst of a minor war. No wonder she was leaving this country with the utmost expedition. Her cabin was on the port side—away from the shooting, at any rate. He considered the group of horsemen who seemed undecided whether to try to keep up with the *Evalina* now that she was in the full current of the Columbia instead of the smaller Okanogan.

Though bullets still splashed into the water occasionally, it was too far to hit anything. He jacked another round into the .45-.90 and sent it their way to encourage a little more distance. Then he went around to the girl's cabin. She had left the door open. He stuck his head in. She was gone. Finally he found her on the starboard side watching the horsemen.

He grabbed her by the arm and jerked her around out of the line of fire. "Don't you know those are real bullets?" he asked.

"But why should they shoot at me?"

Dave shook his head. "You think they can see you or care who they hit? Besides, if you want to ask questions, why are they shooting at me?"

"Yes," the girl said gravely. "Why are they shooting at you, Mr.—"

"Watkins. Dave Watkins. And they're shooting at me because I have something they want."

"Why don't you give it to them?"

Dave stared at the girl. "Why didn't you give your boss what he wanted?" he finally asked.

The girl flushed and looked away. "That's different," she finally said.

"What's different about it? Seems t'me I got as much right to keep my cattle or sell 'em or give 'em away as you got to keep something you hold valuable."

The girl was facing him again. "Are those your cattle down there?"

"They ate my grass and they got my brand on 'em."

"Oh!"

Dave wondered why Miss Emily Jennings or Jenkins or whoever she was seemed so surprised. It seemed almost as if she'd been thinking he was the rustler. There was a solid thunk, and for a moment he thought somebody was chopping wood; then he realized it was just another bullet plowing into the *Evalina*'s sun-toughened superstructure.

He went out onto the side deck and poked a cautious head around to study the right bank. The river was widening and the horsemen were forced still farther away by a bank that was rapidly turning into a cliff. It had to be a lucky shot, he guessed, for they were a mile away and the *Evalina* was gaining, doing all of fifteen miles an hour as her modest speed was added to the Columbia's current. At this rate they'd be in Wenatchee before noon.

He squinted at the knot of riders high on the bluff. There was a puff of black powder smoke and a second later water splashed a hundred yards behind the *Evalina*. The steamer was still erupting sparks and dense black smoke. He guessed the fireman was patching out his seasoned fir with green poplar. Suddenly Dave wondered if they'd had time to take on enough wood for the five-hour run downriver to Wenatchee.

His question was answered when the engine-room telegraph jangled and a moment later the paddlewheel slowed. Dave made his way to the pilothouse. The lean, dyspeptic-looking skipper had tidied up and there was no longer any misshapen-headed corpse in a pepper-and-salt suit. "Where'd you put him?" Dave asked.

The skipper did not take his eyes from the river. He spun the man-high wheel half a turn before jerking a thumb in an "overboard" gesture.

Great, Dave thought. Now how do I go making a report to the authorities with no body? The more he thought about it the worse it looked. He could sympathize with the steamboat man who didn't want his pilothouse all nastied up with dead bodies, but how could he ever find out who was behind it now? If it was that banker in Okanogan . . . Then Dave realized how the law would look at it. Why would honest men toss a body overboard?

5

There was no telegraph up the Okanogan so, barring ship-wreck, Dave knew he could get to Wenatchee well ahead of the news. But sooner or later that hip-pocket sheriff would make his way to Wenatchee and the telegraph. Most proba-bly he would make it before the *Evalina* could complete the five-hundred-mile loop through the badlands to Portland.

"We got enough wood?" Dave asked.

The skipper shrugged and spun the wheel. Dave glanced ahead and realized the river's width at this point meant it was correspondingly shallow. The skipper was steering an erratic course, doing his experienced best not to run aground. Dave left the pilothouse.

John Whitefeather appeared on the side deck. "Bad?" he asked.

Dave shrugged. "If you can find anybody who's not dead tired, see if there's some way to water them."

The older Indian nodded. "I'll be taking a nap in one of the cabins," Dave added, and went to look for an empty bunk. He was nearly asleep when he remembered Emily Jenkins. To hell with her, he decided. It wasn't his boat. The dyspeptic skipper could deal with his own stowaways.

When he woke the *Evalina* was still chuffing sparks and smoke into a cloudless sky. He wiped the sleep from his eyes and tried to guess what time it was. Sun was angling through the tiny cabin window and there was the dank river smell, punctuated with the more vivid odors of cattle below him. They were not bawling too loudly, so he guessed Whitefeather had found some way of watering them.

The sunbeam through the cabin window swept across the bunk and into his eyes again as the *Evalina* rounded another bend. Dave stretched, pulled on his boots, and went out onto the side deck. The country was unchanged: Sparse cheat grass and sagebrush seared beneath the August sun. Dave reflected a moment, realizing that if things had not worked out this way—if those rustlers hadn't come along and loaded his cattle on the steamer for him—he could easily have lost half the herd driving these lean hundred miles down the river.

If there were a ford or a bridge it wouldn't be so bad, but the right bank was granite cliffs and sheer talus slopes for miles on end—typical of the ironies of this western country, where cattle could die of thirst in plain sight of one of the world's largest rivers.

He supposed he had been lucky. Supposed hell! In the natural order of things Dave would have been in jail in Okanogan—or dead at the hands of that affable, whiskey-peddling stranger. He wondered what was going on with that Okanogan banker. Dave's father had done business there since before Dave was born and, though the old man had complained bitterly of gouging interest rates, there had never been any hint of actual banditry. Could the banker be in trouble? Or was he just getting greedy? Or did the railroad own him too?

To hell with it. Dave knew that in any argument before the bench the bank would swing all the weight, buy all the jurors, and . . . The only solution was not to let himself be brought into court. Once he had sold the herd he could pay off the note. And in the future Dave firmly resolved to take his banking business elsewhere. He wondered if he would ever even be able to prove to his own satisfaction that the bank was behind all his troubles.

The *Evalina*'s paddlewheel was turning slowly, barely giving steerageway to pussyfoot through the shallows. Dave studied the sun and guessed it was near noon. He went into the pilothouse where the lean, dyspeptic skipper seemed not to have moved from the man-high wheel since Dave went off to nap. "Where are we?" Dave asked.

"'Bout ten miles north of Wenatchee." The skipper did not take his eyes from the river.

"How about wood?"

The skipper shrugged. "We'll make it."

"Could you make it beyond Wenatchee?"

For the first time the lean man looked at Dave. "I was plannin' on havin' a talk with the sheriff there," he snapped.

It was Dave's turn to shrug. "What good'll that do? You ain't in Okanogan County any more."

The lean man was wrestling with the wheel again. "You just gonna stand by and let them varmints steal my boat and your cattle?" he asked when the *Evalina* had settled down again.

"I don't know what to do," Dave admitted. "But I think we got us a crooked sheriff up home and I don't know what we got down here. You got any idea where we could get in touch with a United States marshal?"

"Portland, maybe."

"You want to waste time and maybe get put in jail by some tinhorn lawman up here?"

The skipper took his eyes from the river momentarily. "What you figurin' on doin'?" He didn't bother waiting for an answer. "Guess I can take on wood at Rock Island. It's only seven or eight miles farther."

Ahead on the right bank of the river, smoke was rising like a plumb line into the cloudless August sky. The *Evalina* pussyfooted another couple of miles through the shallows, and Dave could see the cluster of sun-splintered buildings that was Wenatchee. He went below and stopped halfway down the ladder to survey the tossing sea of horns at his feet. The cattle seemed in good shape so far, but soon they woud be demanding more than water. Even if the steamboat skipper had feed aboard Dave knew the price would be ruinous. They had to get ashore soon and find fresh graze.

He looked about for his Indians and guessed they were trying to catch up on their sleep too. He was back topside heading for the sweltering cabin where he had slept when he encountered Miss Emily Jenkins, still in that all-encompassing tweed traveling suit. Despite the weather she managed somehow to look fresh and wholesome. "I suppose you'll be putting me off at Wenatchee?" She put the accent on the *chee* instead of where it belongs, on the *natch*.

Dave realized that he had completely forgotten about her. "I'm afraid we're not stopping at Wenatchee," he said. To his surprise, the girl did not raise a fuss. If anything, she seemed relieved at this news. Then he remembered that she was on the run too. "What was the name of the man who tried to do you wrong?" he asked.

"My employer was Mr. James Jerome."

The name tugged at Dave's memory. It was one of the monied families on the Okanogan, and he had heard it somewhere in connection with the railroad or maybe it was timber. He was pretty sure there were no Jeromes in the cattle business. "Tried to force himself on you?" he asked conversationally.

"A horrible man," Miss Jenkins said icily. "I don't wish to discuss it."

There was a jangle from the engine-room telegraph, and the *Evalina* began backing. Dave glanced at the right bank. They were opposite the sun-bleached frame houses of Wenatchee. What was that damned teakettle skipper up to? Taking the steps two at a time, Dave lunged topside and into the pilothouse. "I thought we agreed not to stop here!" he snapped.

Wordlessly the dyspeptic skipper pointed. A hundred feet ahead of the *Evalina's* blunt bow something bobbed in the

shallow river. "Just came up out of the mud without warning," the skipper said. "Probably been sunk all winter."

"What is it?" Dave asked. "A log?"

Then, as the steamer drew closer, he saw what it was. Or
what it had been. The skipper looked at him. Dave stared
back. They were in sudden agreement. They had fed the
river a fresh corpse this morning. There was no point in
fishing this one out and losing time in explanations to the
law. From its swollen unrecognizability this body must have
been dead for weeks. As the *Evalina* jangled and began
moving forward again, Dave wondered how many bodies
drifted down this river. Would anybody ever connect him
and the *Evalina* with the man in the pepper-and-salt suit
who had tried to kill Taskoosh?

The body drifted past the portside of the steamer, and
slowly they gained steerageway to thread the shallows past
Wenatchee. The skipper and Dave did not look at each
other. Dave thanked whatever gods that everybody else was
asleep. He had always regarded himself as a law-abiding
man. Suddenly the law up on the Okanogan was forcing him
into a role he had never conceived for himself.

It's only a body, he told himself. Somebody else will find
it and identify it and we don't have time and it's none of my
business and there's no law says I have to waste a day and
put myself in danger just for somebody that's already dead
and . . . And it was wrong. It was against every instinct. He
stumped out of the pilothouse and back up to his cabin.
Maybe he could lie down for a half hour before they
reached Rock Island and began loading wood again.

"What was it?"

He had forgotten the girl. How could he manage so easily
to put a young and attractive woman right out of his mind?
He turned to face the blonde in the tweed traveling suit.
"Oh, uh—dead cow, I guess," he improvised.

Miss Jenkins nodded solemnly. He wondered how she
managed to stand the heat. How could she wear that heavy,

all-encompassing suit and keep from wilting? When he had been a little boy his mother had explained that girls were different. This, he supposed, was one of the differences.

She looked as if she wanted to say something. Dave waited but she didn't speak. Finally he nodded and made his way past her to the cabin where he had been sleeping. Below them cattle bawled, and suddenly he heard the warbling war whoop that was young Dan's happy sound. Dave went into the cabin, lowered himself carefully onto the bunk, and closed his eyes.

What was wrong with him? He had always been a law-abiding man. He hadn't stolen anybody's cattle. He hadn't pulled any swifty with a note that wasn't even due yet. He hadn't tried to rob anybody with funny freight rates. So why was he feeling guilty? Slowly he realized that it wasn't any-thing he hadn't done. Before last night he had never killed a man before. Someday—someday when he could count on an unbought lawman to sort all this out he was going to have to explain why there had been such unseemly haste in dispos-ing of the body of the man he had shot. Maybe somebody who had spent a day on the river in August would under-stand that you couldn't keep dead men around forever. Maybe . . .

Thoughts spun through his head, and he stared with red-rimmed eyes at the ceiling of the cabin. The *Evalina* chuffed stolidly downriver past Wenatchee, and it was midafter-noon. It had taken much longer than he had expected for the teakettle skipper to feel his way down the shallow Co-lumbia. The telegraph jangled again and he felt the boat shudder as the paddlewheel began backing. Now what, he wondered? Then he realized they must be pulling up to the landing at Rock Island.

Abruptly Dave was on his feet, pounding on cabin doors, rousing his Indians. "What happen? Something bad?" Whitefeather asked.

"I hope not," Dave said. "This's where we get off."

"We aren't going to Portland?" Twofingers asked.

Dave shook his head. "There's a telegraph in Wenatchee. I'd just as soon that hip-pocket sheriff goes chasing the *Evalina* downriver. And while he's arranging a reception in Portland we can be on our way somewhere else."

"Seattle!" Dan Sinlahekin's eyes brightened. "I always wanted to see a big town."

"Now what the hell?" the dyspeptic skipper began when they began preparing to unload cattle.

Dave explained to him. The lean man didn't much like it, but he saw the wisdom. "I'll write some letters you can give to the U. S. marshal when you get to Portland," Dave added.

"Yeah, but what about my money?"

"I pay my just debts," Dave said flatly. "You know my brand and you know my range. But when you go figurin' up my bill, just remember I didn't load no cattle on this boat and I didn't agree to anything."

The skipper was suddenly chastened. "I won't hold you up," he said. "And without a load I can make Portland twice as quick. How soon you figure you'll be back?"

"Maybe a year."

"*A year!*" the skipper exploded. "Where in blazes are you goin'?"

"If I don't tell you then nobody's goin' to squeeze it out of you."

So they left it at that after Dave agreed to help the skipper and his crew to load firewood. He left Whitefeather in charge of the cattle who were doing an efficient job of unloading themselves to drink and graze at the narrow band of green along the river's edge. He went out to help the other men load wood.

Finally the skipper guessed he had enough. It was late afternoon now and shadows lengthened to infinity across the low river. They had the last of their gear ashore, and the

Evalina's engineer was encouraging banked fires with seasoned fir. The whistle tooted and the paddlewheel began turning slowly backward. Then abruptly somebody came down the loading apron. It was Miss Emily Jenkins, cool and imperturbable in her tweed traveling suit.

"You can't get off here!" Dave expostulated. "They ain't nothin' here. You ought to ride on down to Portland, where you can get a boat or a train or somethin'."

"I'm going with you, Mr. Watkins."

"No, you ain't! I'm goin' to have enough fun gettin' a herd through them mountains. I ain't ridin' herd on no female!"

Miss Jenkins tilted her blond head quizzically. Behind Dave his Indians stared at this improbable vision in a tweed suit. "Mr. Watkins," she began, "you're absolutely right about my ignorance of the customs of this country. But I wish to avoid an unpleasant pursuit just as I imagine you do. I shall be no hindrance. I'm quite capable of walking as fast as a cow."

"What do you know about cows?" Dave grumped.

"Not very much, Mr. Watkins," she admitted. "But I'm quite sure that even in this peculiar country dead cows floating down rivers do not wear blue serge suits."

6

Even without the presence of Miss Jenkins, who seemed to have no luggage apart from that all-encompassing tweed traveling suit she wore, it would not have been the most satisfactory of camps that evening. Dave had counted on selling a head or two in Wenatchee for supplies. He needed salt. He needed flour. He needed cartridges and baking powder and matches and . . . most of all he needed to be away from the banks of the river, where any passing steamer could see the herd and draw the necessary conclusions.

But it was late and the cattle were hungry and by the time they would be able to drive them away from the scant band of green along the riverbank and get far enough inland across the cheat grass flat to be out of sight it would be dark anyway. Dave gritted his teeth and tried to count his blessings. He was alive. He was not in jail yet. He still had his herd.

So what was he going to do with this female?

John Whitefeather managed not to show it, but Dave suspected the old man was replete with grave amusement. Taskoosh and Twofingers' broad faces were carefully expressionless as they ranged up and down the bank keeping track of the grazing Herefords. Dan Sinlahekin and Kevin Corcoran had already fallen under the spell of this blond goddess, and Dave wondered if it would ever be possible to get any more work out of the boys.

He spurred his gelding to where they squatted, moon-faced and grinning before the girl. "Miss Jenkins," he asked, "do you know how to cook?"

"Yes, Mr. Watkins," the girl said gravely. "Just show me the stove."

"You boys go find some dry wood," Dave instructed. Turning back to the girl, he said, "The kitchen's in Bolly's left-hand pack. This country's got plenty of rocks. Pick whichever you like best for a stove." He spurred off to help Whitefeather turn a steer that seemed determined to lead the herd clear to Portland.

With any kind of luck, Dave decided, Miss Emily Jenkins would take one look at the skillet, the Dutch oven, and the dented coffee pot that were his "kitchen." And after she had considered what can be prepared from flour without salt or baking powder . . . with any kind of luck, by the time he got back from turning those steers Miss Jenkins would be hoofing it the seven or eight miles back to Wenatchee, where she belonged.

By the time he made it to the point Whitefeather had already managed to hoorah the rebellious steers back toward camp. The shadows were blending into darkness now, settling down for the long summer twilight. "Who is she?" the old Indian asked.

"Goldanged if I know," Dave said. "Called herself Emily Jennings and then decided it was Jenkins."

"What's she doing with us?"

Dave explained about the dirty old man who had conned the girl into coming West. "You been around this country longer'n I have, John," he concluded. "You know any James Jerome?"

Whitefeather gave him an odd look. "Don't you?"

"Would I be askin'?"

"I think I know who he is," the old Indian said. "But let's wait till I get a chance to ask the boys."

They rounded a slight headland, and the campfire came in sight. With Twofingers and Taskoosh helping they finally got the herd bedded down and returned to the tiny blaze.

Miss Jenkins had not departed. She had banked coals over the Dutch oven and was boiling something in the skillet. The boys were waiting raptly.

Whitefeather spoke quietly in the old language. Kevin fumbled in his pockets and pulled out a paper in which he had wrapped the remains of several hand-rolled cigarettes. He salvaged the butts and handed John Whitefeather the paper.

John squinted in the firelight. "Can't make it without my glasses," he sighed, and handed the paper to Dave. It was part of the unopened mail he had given the boys to kindle yesterday's breakfast fire. Dave twisted to where he could read in the dim light of the banked sagebrush coals. According to the ornately engraved letterhead, James Jerome was a prominent stockholder, vice president, and principal ornament of the North Valley Bank.

Dave glanced at Whitefeather. "Wish I had your memory," he said, and handed the letter back to young Kevin.

"It's reading," Whitefeather said.

"Huh?"

"I don't remember too good either," the old Indian said. "Man learns to read, he don't have to remember any more. You ought to hear some of the old men reel off tribal history."

Dave had. Though he didn't speak it as much nowadays as they had when he was a kid, Dave knew the old tribal language nearly as well as John Whitefeather. Better, he supposed, than young Sinlahekin and Corcoran. But as iron tools, guns—all the accoutrements of civilization—crept into the country, the words for these new things had slipped into a language that had no words for cartridge or match or locomotive, until at times it seemed as if an English tail were wagging the aboriginal dog.

All of which had nothing to do with the problem of the girl. What was he going to do about Miss Emily Jenkins? She knelt before the fire, and Dave realized with some surprise that the girl had actually built it right: a small fire for cooking instead of those incipient forest fires that most tenderfeet manage to kindle. He wondered what was simmering in the skillet.

It turned out to be dandelion greens with cut-up *cámas* and *wáhpato* roots that the boys had found somewhere along the riverbank. The season was not quite right for the roots, but as Dave devoured them, soaking the liquor into biscuits salted and risen with wood ash, he realized that either he was very hungry or the food was very good. Surveying a profile that even in a tweed traveling suit managed to be interesting, Dave realized that Miss Jenkins possessed hidden depths. "Where'd you learn this kind of cookin'?" he asked.

"There are books that cover the subject quite adequately," the girl replied. "When I knew I was coming out West I endeavored to prepare myself."

They finished eating in thoughtful silence, and the boys lugged tin plates and the remainder of the "kitchen" to a sandspit and scrubbed away at accumulated soot until Miss Jenkins rewarded them with a smile. There was a growing tension, and Dave finally realized the other men were as worried as he about the simple mechanics of living with a woman in camp. Then as the debris of their vegetarian supper was put away, Miss Emily solved the problem by quietly moseying off into the dark.

"Miss Jenkins," Dave called, "can you ride?"

"Not too well in these clothes, Mr. Watkins."

"Well, you better climb onto old Bolly over there," Dave suggested. "I ain't tryin' to scare you, but after dark all the snakes come out o' the rocks and down to the river to drink."

He had expected disbelief, or a minor tantrum. Instead, Miss Jenkins caught the packmare's mane and managed to swing herself womanstyle onto old Bolly's broad back.

By the morning of the second day the boys were no longer reduced to grinning imbeciles each time Miss Jenkins condescended to smile upon them. Dave supposed he ought to pay more attention to the poor girl, but they had climbed steadily over bench after bench, chivvying the herd up the eroded draws that connected one flat with the next until finally there were no more flats, and the cattle were complaining at the sparse grass that appeared here and there where the increasingly vertical ground was not carpeted with pine needles.

Even in August, nights were cold at this altitude, and Miss Jenkins had taken to wrapping up in old Bolly's redolent packsaddle pad to patch out the single blanket that could be spared from Dave's roll. Despite a total lack of luggage, the girl and the tweed suit managed to look as primly pristine as when Dave had first seen her leveling a Deringer on Taskoosh.

Their stores had dwindled so alarmingly that old Bolly had no trouble carrying the girl, who had managed to fold the pack tarp over the sawbuck into a reasonable approximation of a sidesaddle. The trail followed a stream that Whitefeather thought was Peshastin and Twofingers insisted was Swauk Creek.

They had met a grizzled man leading a packhorse and heading East toward Wenatchee the day before who had volunteered no information about himself but 'lowed this was prob'ly the best way to Blewett Pass.

"By the way, Mr. Watkins," the girl asked when the trail widened until she could urge old Bolly up alongside him, "could you tell me where we're going?"

"Seattle, I hope."

"Will your problems end there?"

"Man is born unto trouble," Dave sighed. "And what do you plan on doing once we get through these mountains?"

The girl shrugged. "Perhaps I can find a position."

"Last time I saw Seattle," Dave said, "there was plenty of work for girls, but I don't think you'd much care for that kind of work. You'd best light out for Princeton."

"Providence," Miss Jenkins corrected. "How far away is Seattle?"

Score one for Miss Jenkins. "Oh, uh—120 maybe 150 miles."

"You don't know any closer than that where we are?"

"Well, actually, 'tain't far as the crow flies. But if the crow has to wind round and round these mountains huntin' a way a cow can walk it . . ."

"Is it mountains all the way?"

"Pretty much so. But once we get on t'other side of Blewett Pass there ought to be more graze."

"Oh, dear!"

"What's wrong?"

"I'm sorry. I'm sure it'll be nicer for you but . . ." She hesitated. "If there's more grass I imagine it must rain more."

"Practically nonstop."

"I should have brought an umbrella," Miss Jenkins said.

Dave turned to study the girl. Despite two days on the trail her hair was properly combed. She was clean and her tweed traveling suit unwrinkled. She rode sidesaddle with one knee hooked over the front tree of the sawbuck pack-saddle, decorously showing the toes of her boots from beneath the voluminous skirt. He tried to visualize her popping brush on old Bolly with an umbrella in one hand. Fortunately a whiteface tried to escape up the wrong fork of a canyon and he found an excuse to spur away before his smile degenerated into a belly laugh.

John Whitefeather caught up from where the boys were eating dust. "She's a pretty good cook," he said.

Considering what Miss Jenkins had done with nothing

but flour and whatever the boys could bring her, Dave had to agree. Tonight he resolved that they would eat beef. Veal, at least, since it would be wasteful to watch two thirds of a cow spoil before they could eat it. There was a maverick, out-of-season calf that wouldn't bring much money anyhow.

"She rides a horse pretty good too," Whitefeather added.

The old Indian had been around whites so long that he would occasionally come right out and make a direct statement like this. Dave grinned. "You're too old and I'm too young," he said. "What you talkin' her up for?"

"Neither half of that's true," Whitefeather said with a hint of amusement, "but I was just wondering if you could really learn all that out of a book."

Abruptly Dave realized the older man was still reasoning in an eliptical Indian fashion after all. "Do you know somethin' I don't know?" he asked.

"Wouldn't be hard now, would it?"

Dave sighed. Whitefeather was right. He didn't know the first thing about Miss Emily Jennings or Jenkins or whoever it was who had appeared from nowhere and attached herself to them. He studied the sun filtering down through the spruce and wondered how far they were from Wenatchee. Had that hip-pocket sheriff gotten down there to the telegraph yet? Had he already discovered that Dave and his cattle were not floating downriver toward Portland? How much longer would it take to get through these mountains and drive a herd through the swamps and around the lakes, and across the creeks and rivers to Seattle? And once they had made it to Seattle?

They had traveled undisturbed for two days. After all the hell he'd had getting out of the Okanogan, Dave found the relative peace unreal: two whole days with nothing to do but drive himself and his men to boneweariness hoorahing cattle up through these mountains. The trail widened, and old Bolly moved up to join them. Still looking as if she had just stepped off the boat, Miss Emily bestowed a dazzling smile on old Whitefeather.

Dave felt a tiny twinge of annoyance. He was the boss of this oufit. He had allowed her to join their party. Yet Miss Jennings or Jenkins had never bestowed such a smile upon him.

Whitefeather's weathered face broke into a smile as brilliant as Miss Emily's. The older man tipped his broad-brimmed hat and had to rearrange the cord beneath his braids. Fiddling with his hat, he asked, "Have you always ridden sidesaddle, Miss Jerome?"

"No," the girl said. "I can ride western style when I have suitable attire—a divided skirt."

Dave gasped and looked quickly away. *Miss Jerome!* He got his face under control and turned back, looking for some sign that the girl realized she had given herself away. *Jerome.* Wasn't that the name Whitefeather had shown him on the bank's letterhead? Of course it was. Why was he trying to pretend—wishing it wasn't so?

"You're also an excellent cook, Miss Jerome," Whitefeather added, breaking out words Dave had never heard the laconic old man use before.

"Mr. Jerome was my employer," the girl said, her face smooth and untroubled. "I am Emily Jenkins."

John Whitefeather solemnly nodded. "I stand corrected," he said.

7

A week passed and though the girl remained pristine as an ad for Miss Phoebe Snow, her tweed traveling suit began to show hints of usage. The wear was more apparent on Dave and his Indians, but the cattle—at the expense of the men—were still fat and fit as they crossed the summit of Snoqualmie, which is the second-highest pass on the road to Seattle, some six strenuous days across the high country from Blewett.

The land was greener now and they were becoming inured to the sudden showers where the west wind dumped its moisture on the windward side of the mountains.

"Ever get to Seattle and get some money I get me a slicker," John Whitefeather said.

"And some gum boots," Taskoosh added.

Heading downhill from the Snoqualmie summit, they entered rolling country filled with pines and firs, dotted with lakes and miles-wide barrages of rain forest where the ferns and wild blackberries grew in masses penetrable to nothing larger than the countless garter snakes on which autumn-fat bears topped off for their winter sleep.

Dave gave silent thanks for the snakes which, with blackberries for dessert, seemed more attractive to the bears than were his cattle. Bolly appeared alongside his gelding. Dave turned to Miss Emily, who sat much lower on the packhorse, thanks to totally exhausted supplies. "How much farther?" she asked.

Dave shrugged. "Maybe fifty miles."

"Is it true that you're going to Alaska?"

Dave was startled out of his reverie. "Who told you that?"

It was Miss Emily's turn to shrug.

"No," Dave said. "I thought about it, but it's a crazy idea. Country's impossible, and how'd I ever get up there in the first place?"

"Then what are you going to do in Seattle?"

"Sell this herd and pay off my debts."

The trail narrowed again, and Miss Emily's packhorse dropped behind, leaving Dave with the unspoken question. *If he could sell the herd . . .* Ever since '93 things had been going to hell, beef prices dropping, hide prices dropping— everything going rock bottom except the cost of living. And in 1896 and '97 the plummeting economy had taken a sudden, even sharper downturn. There was a strong possibility that when they reached Seattle all Dave's old troubles would be there plus, possibly, a few new ones if the banker and that hip-pocket sheriff in Okanogan had outguessed him.

"Smoke!" It was young Sinlahekin shouting from up at the point. Dave wondered what the boy was doing up there when he should have been eating dust, but the question was forgotten in the sudden fear that surged through Dave before he realized that with all the rain they'd been getting there existed scant danger of forest fire. He got around the herd and saw the smoke ahead.

Some five miles down the lush, grassy valley a single plume of smoke rose vertically from a log cabin. It was the first human sign they had seen since the close-mouthed stranger over a week ago had reluctantly 'lowed they were on the best road for Blewett.

The bawling herd drew nearer, and Dave began planning how to get them around the scraggly garden that lay behind a zigzag rail fence with whole sections collapsed. John Whitefeather rode up. "Bad?" he asked.

It would be, Dave knew, if his cattle managed to get in and trample that excuse for a garden. Anybody on the fringes of civilization was liable to be a trifle woodsy to begin with, and there had never been that much good feeling between cattlemen and sodbusters to start with.

They began chivvying the cattle down the opposite side of the narrow valley, and at the worst possible moment young Dan and Kevin lost control. The herd surged toward the garden and the decrepit cabin. There was a sudden thundering of hooves as Dave and the others struggled to turn them. Then abruptly he saw a haggard woman in the breached fence flapping an apron. In the next breach Miss Emily stood shrieking lustily as she waved a scrap of tarp.

With a sudden sick feeling Dave wondered if there would remain enough of either woman to bury. The herd thundered toward them and the garden. He struggled to get through, yelling futilely into the noise of pounding hooves. Then abruptly the lead steers spun and the herd was milling in confusion.

Finally the cattle were past the garden. Dave spurred his mount back to where Emily and the other woman waited in the garden. Weak-kneed with relief, he was afraid to dismount lest he betray himself. "You must set a lot of store by that garden, ma'am," he finally managed.

"I got to," the haggard woman said, "since my man skun out for Alaska and left me with a passel o' young'uns."

"Maybe we could—" Then he saw that Miss Emily had already undone the pack on old Bolly and was preparing to give away half their fresh meat before it could spoil. Hastily, Dave spurred on after the herd.

That night as they gorged themselves on carrots and new potatoes he said, "Don't you know a herd of cows can kill anybody on foot?"

Miss Emily looked up from her tin plate, and for the first

time Dave saw lines of fatigue on her thinning face. "I've heard so, Mr. Watkins," she said. "But if travel through these mountains fails to do for me, then I may be indestructible."

Dave nodded soberly, wondering what the girl would do once they reached Seattle.

They were camped beside a lake in lush meadow that seemed a test plot for some bovine heaven. The cattle had eaten their fill and bedded down on the grassy flat between lake and pine. The spot might have been heaven for humans —had it not been for the mosquitos that buzzed unscathed through the smudge that the boys had lit upwind. They were five miles down the valley from the haggard woman's garden and had already passed one other farm. From now on life would turn into a constant struggle to keep the herd off somebody's planted field and keep an irate farmer from opening up on them with whatever arms available.

There was a faint smell in the air that Dave couldn't quite make out; then abruptly he realized it was coal smoke. Moments later he caught the distant quilling squall of a locomotive whistle. The boys pricked up their ears and looked at Dave. He shrugged. It made little difference if the train were ten miles or ten feet away; he had no money, and he wasn't about to give the railroad any legal handle on his herd. As they rolled up to sleep in the drifting cloud of smoke he heard the mournful wail of another steam train.

Next day Dave tried to keep his forebodings to himself. His Indians were looking forward to Seattle—bright lights and a holiday. He didn't know if he would be able to scrape up even enough money to buy a sack of flour and get off this unsatisfying diet of beef and wild asparagus, blackberries, *cámas*— Damn! What wouldn't he give for just one decent biscuit!

John Whitefeather edged his horse closer. "Bad?" he asked.

Dave sighed and tried to shrug off his depression. "We'll

make out somehow," he promised. But if he was depressed here, what had ever gotten into him to think of Alaska? To take cattle that far north, even in summer, was impossible. He had to sell the herd in Seattle.

Another day and they were driving cattle through the squishy, semiliquid mud of North Bend's only street. "Flour?" the single grocer asked. "Sure, I'll sell you flour. But I can't trade for beef. Ain't nobody in this town'd be able to buy it afore it spoilt."

So they pushed on another day through increasing rain, now stopping occasionally to pull mired cows from the muddy banks of lakes and streams. Miss Emily had rigged the tarp of old Bolly's empty pack into a miniature tent and ranged ahead of the herd now that they were in more civilized country. When Dave realized with an abrupt shock that he had not seen her for over four hours he was not worried—only resigned.

Now that Seattle was only a day's hard ride away he wondered if he would ever see his packsaddle or old Bolly again. He struggled to be philosophical about it. The girl had worked her passage. She had turned into a surprisingly competent cook, foraging as ably as any squaw for roots and berries. Perhaps she had earned an old horse and an older packsaddle. But he couldn't get the mysterious Miss Jennings or Jenkins or Jerome or whatever her name was out of his mind. He struggled to forget her. Anyone as quietly competent as Miss Emily would not be defeated by Seattle.

Dave had not voiced his concern, but soon he realized that the girl's absence had infected everyone with a nagging worry. The boys found constant excuses to range ahead of the herd instead of behind, where they belonged. Even old Whitefeather seemed to be paying more attention to the country in front of them than was strictly necessary. Finally he dropped back to where Dave was managing to contain one side of the herd.

"What you think?" the old Indian asked.

Dave didn't bother playing innocent. "She'll survive," he said.

Whitefeather gave him an inscrutable look. "Yeah," he said, and spurred off after a wandering steer. The rain changed from heavy to heavier. Clothing and bedrolls had not dried properly for days. It had to be just the rain, Dave told himself. This abominable coastal weather was enough to give anybody the willies. But despite the incessant rain and despite their lean prospects, the camp had been a happy place until Miss Emily had disappeared.

She had been gone four or five hours now, he realized. Young Dan and Kevin were coming back from the point. "Tracks," Kevin said.

Dave wondered if the question had been that plain on his face. "What kind of tracks?" he bluffed. The boys gave him an odd look, and Dave wondered who had ever invented the libel that Indians were inscrutable.

His reverie was cut off by a new emergency. A strange cowboy appeared in the distance where they had been pretending not to look for Miss Emily. Dave had been rehearsing suitably casual ways to ask if anyone had seen a young lady in a tweed traveling suit on a packhorse when still another cowboy appeared, and it was suddenly apparent that some outfit was driving cattle in the opposite direction. Cattle herds being even less maneuverable than liners at sea, there would be a collision in minutes, followed by perhaps days of sorting out brands and all manner of unpleasantness.

Whooping and hoorahing, waving the piece of tarp he had been using for a rain shelter, Dave galloped along the edge of his cows, struggling to keep a distance between the two herds. Ahead the strange cowboys were struggling with equal intensity to keep the moving masses of Herefords separated.

"Oh, goddamn!" John Whitefeather was wailing with a perfect scrutability as he tore off to slap a rope end over the rump of a steer that sought romance and fulfillment in the other herd. Taskoosh and Twofingers were shrieking in falsetto excitement, and over the thunder of horses and cattle Dave could hear Sinlahekin's war whoop loud and clear.

Ponderously, the herds passed one another, men from both outfits ignoring the far flanks to keep some separation between them.

The valley at this point was some three miles from stream to foothills. Even if they managed to pass without mixing the herds it would take the rest of the day to round up strays.

It turned out to be a long afternoon, and the rain did not cease even momentarily. Finally there was a decent distance between the herds, and Dave sent the boys ahead to stop the leaders and see if it was possible to get his cattle bedded down for the night. Dave was trotting once more to the rear when he saw a man coming toward him mounted on a sorrel studhorse. It was not one of Dave's people.

"Howdy," the stranger said. "Headin' for Seattle?"

Dave nodded. He had been too busy to dwell on the significance of a herd heading the opposite way. "You comin' from that way?" It was an obvious question.

The stranger nodded. "Hung around a week," he said.

Dave felt his stomach suddenly emptier than usual. "That bad?" he asked. "What're they payin'?"

The red-headed stranger offered a chaw that Dave declined with thanks. "'Cordin' to the paper, milkers are twenty-five eighty-five," he said. "Beef's eighteen sixty-one."

Dave's stomach twisted and roiled emptily. It was even worse than he had expected. "But how come you didn't take it?" he asked. "Where you headin' now?"

The stranger masticated his mouthful of cut plug and spat brown juice before answering. "That's what the paper said," he explained. "But I hung around the stockyards a week and nobody ever came around to buy."

Dave stared.

"Ain't nothin' to do but go home," the red-haired stranger

said. "Every damn fool and his brother in Seattle's gone tearin' off to Alaska. Ain't nobody left to work the slaughterhouse."

"Oh." It made sense but it offered no solution. Dave wondered what he was going to do now. For several moments he didn't even think about Miss Emily.

8

Camp was grim and cheerless that night as they spitted strips of beef that was beginning to turn, sitting solemnly in a circle around a fire of damp wood, each trying to brown the strip of beef wrapped around his green stick. Along with Miss Emily and old Bolly, their kitchen had departed too—which made scant difference, since they had nothing to eat but the beef old Whitefeather had been carrying. Dave supposed the girl would be in Seattle by now, doing whatever it was that enterprising young women do in strange towns. Somehow he hadn't thought it of her.

They were wet and miserable as they ate in wan exhaustion, each thinking the same thought. Bolly's hoofprints had stood out like signposts in the mud until the red-haired stranger had come along to chop that trail with the prints of half a thousand Herefords. So what, Dave thought. They might track her to Seattle, but once there the girl could disappear. Hadn't that been exactly what he wanted? He had problems enough without taking on the responsibility of a young woman, no matter how blond, how smooth-skinned, how . . .

They shivered through the night in wet blankets and finally got up, too dispirited to breakfast on more turning meat. Splashing through the puddles of some nameless town a few miles east, so the resident whittler told them, of Issaquah, Dave guessed if his stomach held out they could reach Seattle in two more days. And then what? Could they perhaps butcher one cow and go from house to house bartering for flour enough to satiate his craving for just one biscuit?

This morning the rain sometimes stopped for five minutes at a time. Dave rode along the left edge of the herd, wondering if it were humanly possible to be more miserable, when he saw another cabin. It was difficult to believe anyone could inhabit so decrepit a structure. One end of the roof had collapsed completely. Yet smoke rose from a metal pipe at the other end, hesitating momentarily before it curled down to "stool" like winter wheat. He was thinking dismally of one more garden to avoid when a hobbled horse came from behind the cabin. It was Bolly.

Dave struggled to control conflicting emotions. The boys were under no such inhibition as they spurred ahead to greet the slight figure in herringbone tweed traveling suit who appeared in the doorway of the ruined cabin. "Well, Mr. Watkins, what held you up?" she asked.

Dave mumbled an explanation about the herd coming in the opposite direction. There were appetizing smells from behind her inside the ruined cabin. Dave was willing to swear he could smell biscuits. He knew he could smell coffee for the first time in more than two weeks.

Cattle were already grazing among the volunteer potatoes that sprang untended from a long-abandoned garden. Though it was still forenoon, by unspoken agreement they called it a day and crowded into the cabin. In the reasonably rainproof half of the ruined structure Miss Emily had strung the ropes from Bolly's packsaddle and was drying blankets. Poking through them in the dark interior of the cabin, Dave's hand encountered a hidden hoard of feminine things drying. Hastily he withdrew and tried to concentrate on the smell of biscuits baking.

Despite having done without biscuits and coffee for

longer than he liked to remember, Dave found his thoughts creeping uncontrollably back to that clutch of lacy things drying between the blankets and the concomitant conjecture that several layers must be missing between the herringbone tweed traveling suit and the newly washed skin that peeped from collar and cuff. He strung his lariat and began hanging his own sodden blankets.

In the suddenly festive atmosphere nobody thought to wonder where fresh coffee and flour for biscuits had come from. Dave found himself avoiding the question as skittishly as he tried not to think about what lay between the tweed suit and Miss Emily. John Whitefeather just happened to be looking directly at Dave when young Sinlahekin voiced the question.

"Where'd you get the money for groceries, Miss Emily?" the young Indian asked.

"When I left Mr. Jerome's employ I had some small funds of my own, which I was saving for a suitable occasion."

From the amusement in Whitefeather's broad, dark face, Dave deduced that his own face must have been all too readable.

That night the steady rain outdid itself with orchestral accompaniments of thunder and lightning, which kept them busy half the night controlling the herd. Even so, with a partial roof, with a fireplace, with real food and half-dry blankets for a change, their spirits were revived.

Morning dawned bright and clear for the first time in a fortnight. Saddling up, Dave noted that John Whitefeather was gone. At first he assumed the older man was off doing what men do alone in the bushes, but when Whitefeather's hobbled mount was still unsaddled fifteen minutes later after Dave's morning circuit of the herd, he began to worry.

He found the old man chanting softly as he soaped and washed his braids in a rain-swollen creek below the cabin. Dave knew better than to interrupt. Silently he withdrew and went back to getting the herd on the move. At peace with himself, the older Indian appeared a half hour later.

"Did you stop it?" Dave asked, pointing toward the cloudless sky.

Whitefeather gave him the sheepish look of a Christian caught backsliding and said nothing. For once it was Dave's turn to be amused, but instead he found himself wondering just what had finally changed the weather.

They made up for lost time as the ground dried and hardened until on the morning of the second day A.B., After Biscuits, as Dave would always remember it, the smokes of Seattle's several thousand wood and coal stoves rose in the distance.

Dan Sinlahekin emitted the war whoop that was his happy sound. Dave's spirits rose in spite of the red-haired stranger's warning. Surely in a city this size somebody must have an appetite for beef—and a pocket to pay for it.

If he hadn't gotten his directions mixed up they still had to bear south to get around Lake Washington, then north again by the coal mine near Renton. Somewhere along the Duwamish River, which was sometimes bank-to-bank with logs awaiting the sawmill, was a slaughterhouse before he would even reach the city stockyards. Dave wondered if the red-haired, tobacco-chewing man had known about that one. More to the point, he wondered if it was still there, still open after all this time.

Old Bolly came alongside. Dave turned to face the girl. "Well, Miss," he said with sudden awkwardness, "I suppose you'll be leaving us here, headin' back to Boston?"

"It's Providence, Mr. Watkins." She hesitated a moment. "My plans at present are unsettled. However, I'm sure we've still time tomorrow for farewells." She smiled at Dave for the first time in several days, and he wondered why suddenly he felt so much better.

His buoyant spirits lasted all afternoon and even into the

following day when they had finally threaded the herd through Renton and the dozen other clusters of houses that would someday be towns on the way into the south end of Seattle. It had been nearly four years since his only brief visit to Seattle. The city had grown beyond recognition, and he knew even before he arrived that the ramshackle slaughterhouse he remembered would have burned down or been torn down to make room for more houses.

Yet despite all the new houses there was an odd air of paralysis—as if everything had abruptly stopped in mid-boom. There were half-built houses that would never be finished. There were empty houses. There were piles of rain-soaked ashes that had once been houses. Lawns and gardens had gone back to bramble and skunk cabbage as the rain forest struggled to reclaim disputed territory.

Over all lay the redolent stink of sawdust, of fresh sawn, unpainted lumber punctuated with the acrid smoke from those round brick monuments to waste that solved the rubbish problem at hundreds of sawmills.

They came to a crossroads and halted, the herd bawling and milling about a general store. Dave had come too far already. The slaughterhouse he remembered was gone. If he kept on to the stockyards—and if the red-haired puncher had been telling the truth, Dave realized he might end up being stuck for a feed bill he could ill afford.

The grocer, a small harassed-looking man, appeared in the doorway of his store. He took one look at the herd, shrugged as if bawling critters besieged him every day and twice on Saturdays, before going back inside and closing the door.

Dave forced his way through and tied his mount at the hitching rail. "Yes, sir, need something?" the grocer asked hopefully when he entered.

Dave studied the "hay, feed, groceries" sign. "Sure do," he said. "Mostly I need some money."

"Welcome to the club," the small man said sourly.

"That bad?" Dave asked.

"Worse."

"Whatever happened to that slaughterhouse used to be a mile or so up the road?"

"Burned down." The small man hesitated a moment, then by way of explanation added, "With unpainted wood and cedar shingle roofs and every chimney in town shooting pine rosin sparks, it's a wonder the whole town doesn't burn down oftener."

"Is that what happened?"

"Not lately. Trouble now is this town's full of drifters tryin' to make it to Alaska. Only they ain't got a dime among them, and anybody has is already off and gone."

"Business ought to be good," Dave hazarded.

"Would be if I could just get to Alaska," the small man said. "I still got enough stock to clean up. Trouble is, if I don't come up with some cash money in two weeks the bank's gonna git it all." He sighed. "Storekeepin' here's bad as sellin' coal in Vancouver."

Dave smiled to conceal his ignorance. "Any place I can put them critters for a day or two?" he finally asked.

"Help yourself. More grass in a mile here than there is in fifty anywhere else in the world."

Which explained why beef was so cheap. What it did not explain was what to do now, Dave realized. He exchanged a few more pleasantries with the despondent grocer and went out to see about bedding down the cattle. "We gonna stay here?" Whitefeather asked.

"For a while," Dave said. "At least till I can ride into town and see what's going on."

"Who cares what's going on?" Whitefeather asked. "Sell your cattle and get out of this den of iniquity before—" He broke off with a foreboding look at the boys, who were bubbling over with excitement at their first sight of a city.

Dave explained about the dying cattle market. John Whitefeather's broad, dark face became more worried. "I'll try to keep them here," he promised. As Dave mounted his gelding for the ten-mile trot downtown, he sensed that something was different. It wasn't until he was halfway into town that he realized that old Bolly and Miss Emily had once more disappeared.

To hell with it. The girl had displayed an ample ability to take care of herself. And she had said there would be time later for farewells. Then he realized this might have been her diplomatic way of saying good-bye. He sighed and shrugged again.

There was a groaning, grinding noise behind him like a giant coffee mill. Dave and his horse turned their heads at the same time. Dave had seen an electric streetcar before. His horse had never seen one of these sparking, grinding, bell-clanging monstrosities.

The motorman and several passengers watched with a mixture of amusement and impatience to see whether Dave would remain aboard the saddle that his gelding was abruptly trying to shake off. For half a minute it was a near thing; then Dave managed to get the flighty gelding to settle down. Half a hundred tobacco chewers had emerged from the swinging doors of a saloon to see whether man, horse, or streetcar would win.

Dave spurred toward them, and the gawkers scattered. He tied to the rail before the saloon, wishing he had the price of a drink—by which he meant he wished he could spare it, for Dave had nearly half a dollar in his pocket. He considered the streetcar tracks and remembered that the last time he had been here there had been three separate cable car lines groaning and clanking up the hill between Elliott Bay and Lake Washington.

But if he left his horse tied here . . . Dave's dilemma was temporarily solved when he noted the "telephone" sign above the swinging doors. Giving the gawkers a careful, face-memorizing look, he went in and asked the bartender where the phone was.

The balding, handlebar-mustached man pointed at the far wall. Dave spent a moment studying the immense instrument. He looked through the directory and could find nothing. Finally he dropped a nickel into the slot and asked the girl to connect him with the stockyards.

"I'm sorry, sir. That number does not answer."

"But there *is* a number? They've got a telephone?"

"Oh, yes, sir. Would you like the number?"

"Would it do me any good?"

The mechanical voice unbent momentarily. "I don't think so," the girl said. "Nobody's been answering there for a couple of weeks."

So that was that. He tried to shrug it off, saying he'd known it all the time or at least ever since the red-haired stranger driving a herd in the opposite direction had warned him. But this time there was no fleeting hope—no way to sell his cattle. He fingered the forty-odd cents in his pocket and went outside where a half-dozen gawkers still looked covetously at his gelding. Dave wondered if it was the horse or the rider that discouraged them. Searching the street carefully for another tramcar, he mounted and headed back where he had left his Indians.

It was turning dark when he got back to where they had settled into one of the abandoned houses. He saw Bolly standing in the yard and was unaccountably cheered at the knowledge that Miss Emily had returned after all. Then as he came closer he saw that all five of his people clustered around old Bolly, ignoring the herd. The herd was bedded down but, damn it, why was nobody tending to business? He spurred up, and John Whitefeather turned to greet him. "Bad," the old Indian said.

"What's bad?" Dave demanded.

Whitefeather pointed at Bolly's packsaddle still wrapped

with the tarp Miss Emily had used to rig a sidesaddle. Hanging from one of the crisscrossing ropes was a large fragment of torn lace. Dave suddenly knew that this was all of Miss Emily that had come home.

9

"Only got here a minute before you did," Whitefeather said. "You think she's hurt?"

Dave didn't. The girl had ridden this placid old mare through the mountains perched atop a heap of supplies. Bolly would not indulge in any fireworks even if someone were to fire a cannon behind her, much less a streetcar. He studied the lace, remembering how carefully proper the girl had concealed these things to dry between blankets. He cringed at the thought of the poor girl's mortification if ever she were to learn how they had all stood here gawking at something that was no man's business.

For the girl to have been bucked off just didn't make sense. Nor, Dave realized, did it make sense for a piece of lace to be torn in just this fashion. It wasn't as if it had snagged on brambles or barbed wire. The lace was stuffed beneath one of the ropes that crisscrossed the tarp and sawbuck to create a makeshift sidesaddle—almost as if someone had put it there.

The girl had been with them for better than three weeks now. Dave reflected on how little he actually knew about Miss Emily Jennings-Jenkins or whatever. . . . But as he reflected on the paucity of his knowledge about the girl he became gradually sure of one thing. Miss Emily was a competent rider, and no matter what one might accuse her of, no one could ever hint that Miss Emily was stupid. She concealed her underwear to dry between blankets or a pillow case, as any properly raised young lady was taught.

If there was a great strip of lace stuffed under a rope in plain sight for all of them to gawk at, there was a reason for it. There was only one thing Dave could think of that would make a girl do such an unlikely thing. "She's tryin' to tell us somethin'," he said.

"What?"

"Well," Dave reflected, "if she had been bucked off, there's people all over this country. She'd've sent word somehow."

Five Indians hung on his every word. Dave hesitated, afraid of sounding foolish. But there was just no other reason he could think of. "Miss Emily's been kidnaped," he said.

Had he been of a more reflective turn of mind and with fewer things on his mind at the moment, Dave might have been amused at the awestruck expressions this remark elicited.

"No kiddin'? But what for?" Kevin asked.

John Whitefeather gave the boy a pitying glance.

"Someday when you're older," Twofingers said. Kevin Corcoran's broad, dark face flushed even darker.

Dave hesitated. Something had to be done. He remembered the singular incompetence of the local police, who were too busy arresting cowboys, fishermen, and loggers to do anything about the businessmen who furnished boisterous, lonely men with poisoned whiskey and poisoned girls.

Dave had been so involved with his own uncertain future that he had carefully avoided thinking too deeply about the girl. Emily Jennings or Jenkins, blond, twenty-four. This town would hold plenty of men not so hesitant to . . . But Miss Emily, Dave was ready to swear, was not that kind of a girl. On the trail under the most difficult circumstances she had worked hard, done more than her share when another kind of woman would have turned it into a picnic, forced his men into a murderous competition, and . . . Dave sighed. There was something unexplained about Miss Emily, but any girl who could produce a meal with hot biscuits at the lowest point of a low trip—any girl who had been raised to dry her underwear out of sight . . .

"John," he said, turning to Whitefeather, "you and the boys stay here and keep an eye on the herd. Taskoosh better stay too. Twofingers can come with me."

"Where we goin'?" Hodge Twofingers asked.

"To look for Miss Emily."

Within minutes they had saddled up and were trotting back into town. Dave struggled to control his impatience. He wanted to gallop his gelding, but the beast had already done over twenty miles today and there might be a need later for an unexhausted horse. They passed the end of the streetcar line, and he warned Twofingers about the sparking, groaning monsters. They passed the saloon, now murkily lit with coal oil lamps. They reached the downtown section of Seattle, which is oddly contained between Elliott Bay and Lake Washington, with suburbs expanding to north and south like the twin bulges of an hourglass.

Twenty years ago Yesler Way had been a muddy ditch down which to skid logs to the sawmill. Now it was paved with red brick and adorned with a cable car that went up over the hill between lake and bay. Despite these improvements everyone still called it Skid Road. Looking up and down the row of saloons, brothels, and cheap lodgings, Dave understood for the first time why Skid Road was beginning to have a new meaning.

Where to begin in this cross section of hell? Drunken fishermen in watch caps and oilskins vied with loggers not averse to kicking with spiked boots for the favors of the Skid Road harlots, encouraged by the poisonous concoctions of inventive saloonkeepers. Here and there sleek and dangerous-looking men in derby hats moved in pairs, buying sailors, fishermen, and loggers drinks.

Though Seattle as a whole might be in the doldrums, this section, which catered to the needs of transient men, was very busy. Dave hesitated before a building. Windows opened. Painted women whistled and beckoned from upstairs. Hodge Twofingers stared at Dave with scandalized astonishment. "White preachers all the time saying *we* shouldn't do this," he grumbled. "Talk about forked tongues!"

"Wait here," Dave said. Seattle was an odd place—full of coastal Siwash but with the usual double standard when it came to drinking and fornication. He wanted to save time and spare Twofingers embarrassment.

"You goin' *in* there?" the Indian asked.

"Got to start askin' somewhere," Dave said.

"I'm lookin' for a girl," he explained to the hennaed horror who greeted him.

"You've come to the right place," the madam assured him.

"Uh—not just any girl," Dave amended.

"Of course not," she agreed. "Our girls are all something special."

Dave sighed and started over.

"Sorry," the red-dyed madam said. "Why should I go in for kidnaping when there are more volunteers than I can use?" She shrugged and added, "You know, the only real fate worse than death is slow starvation."

Dave went back out onto the street, and Twofingers was gone. Glancing up and down the street, he saw the Indian's back. He was walking between two men in blue serge suits and low-crowned derbys. Dave hastened up behind them and tapped the pair of strangers on the shoulders. As they turned he put his hands to his belt, hitching up his jacket. "That one belongs to me," he said.

The strangers looked dangerous for a moment, then decided this tall stranger might be more so. They shrugged and walked off, leaving Twofingers.

"What'd they tell you?" Dave asked.

"Nothin'. Just asked me if I wanted a drink."

"We didn't come here to drink!" Dave snapped.

They mounted their horses and began the slow walk up Skid Road, looking for some hint of Miss Emily. It was, Dave realized, a hopeless task. He gave Twofingers an enlightening lecture on the practice of crimping and left the Indian to watch their horses while he entered another establishment where painted women beckoned.

This time the madam was more sympathetic. "I haven't heard anything," she said, "but I suppose it must happen. Where can I reach you for the reward?" She paused. "Stealing girls is like selling coal in Vancouver." Dave had always thought it was Newcastle. He gave her the name and address of the storekeeper where his herd was pasturing. This time Twofingers still held the horses when he came outside. They went up the length of Yesler Way and down Madison Street offering a reward for any information about an attractive blonde, about twenty-four, wearing a well-worn herringbone tweed traveling suit. *And torn underwear*, Dave wanted to add, but he could not bring himself to talk that way about Miss Emily.

"You think this's gonna do any good?" Twofingers asked, waving at the endless rows of brothels.

Dave didn't. But what else could he do? If an offer of fifty dollars couldn't flush Miss Emily's kidnapers out of the woodwork, nothing could. Once he had the girl alive and safe again there would be time to wonder where and how he was ever going to scrape up that kind of money.

It must have been nearing midnight when Dave despairingly realized he had done all that was humanly possible for a stranger in the big city to do. Loggers in caulk boots, fishermen, would-be gold miners still thronged Skid Road when they finally gave up and spurred their horses south on First Avenue. It was Hodge Twofingers who first saw the small sign. Studying it, Dave realized there was still something else he could do to find Miss Emily.

They dismounted, ground tying their horses to study the inconspicuous sign over the closed door. The sign was eloquently noncommittal. It said PINKERTON's. Dave tried the door. It was locked. He could see a faint glow of lamplight around the curtain. He was putting out a hand to knock when abruptly he realized a detective agency was not going to be taken in with promises of rewards. These hard-nosed professionals would want their money—retainer, they'd probably call it—but no matter what they called it, it would be cash on the barrelhead and in advance.

He was turning away when he heard angry voices inside. One of them was female. Couldn't be, he knew. But that voice sounded awfully familiar. Dave sensed he was grasp-ing at straws, but when he turned in the dimly lit street Twofingers was already silently oozing over a low fence and around to a sidewindow. Dave followed him and joined the Indian to squint into a window where the blind was torn and there was just a chance that they might be able to make out who . . .

It was dark in the side yard. Out in the street his ground-tied gelding whinnied. Dave guessed he should have left the horse farther away. It was too damn dark. He stumbled and caught himself just in time not to knock over a half-dozen boards that leaned against the wall of the Pinkertons.

Then suddenly there was entirely too much light. Roman candles and skyrockets exploded inside his head. Ball light-ning darted wildly and then he was falling, spinning back-ward and down a deep, dark hole. As he fell, still spinning and sinking, he wondered if he had really caught a glimpse of Miss Emily through the torn curtain, or was he just imag-ining it?

10

Later, when he was in a more analytical frame of mind, Dave would suppose he had been unconscious for a while, but at the time he sensed no gap. He had been sinking backward, rolling and spinning down into a dark hole, and now it seemed that he had been rocking and tumbling for an unconscionably long time.

There was an odd, rhythmic creaking. He shivered and realized that his clothing was damp. He tried to move and could not. He opened his eyes and for one panic-stricken moment thought he was blind. Then he sensed a tarp over his face. He lay face up inside what felt very like a barrel.

The barrel seemed to be rocking with a beat that had no relationship to the rhythmic, groaning noise. Each time it moved his head rolled slightly, and each time his head rolled it throbbed until he felt as if it were going to fly off. He struggled to move again, and a sudden wave of total pain surged through him.

Sinking back down into an abyss of oblivion, he realized that somewhere around him water was gurgling and flowing. Another small eternity passed, and then very gradually Dave knew he was no longer unconscious, that he was neither blind nor paralyzed. He lay beneath a tarp, bound too tight to think about moving even if he had been possessed of a clear head. He was not in any barrel, he understood now. He had been tossed into the bow of a round-bottomed boat. The rhythmic groaning noise and accompanying splashes came from a pair of oars.

With a marvelous illogicality, his first thought was not for his own safety. Instead, he wondered if his gelding would have sense enough to go home. The beast was skittish enough not to let any stranger mount. He had ground tied it, so maybe the horse would be back with his Indians by now, furnishing them with another cryptic message, just as old Bolly had.

"That you, Mike?" It was a curiously muted kind of yell—as if somebody wished he were whispering. There was a grunt from closer at hand, and the groaning of oarlocks ceased. A moment later Dave felt the pulling boat thud against something. There were muttered curses and tramping footsteps, then he heard a shrill squealing. It took Dave a while to recognize the sound of rope passing through an ungreased pulley.

More thumpings and fumblings, more goddamnits, and the pulley squealed again. It squealed twice more and then the tarp was jerked from Dave. He tried to see, but the sky was black and spinning crazily. Rough hands turned him over, and suddenly he was being lifted from the pulling boat. He spun crazily in the air for a minute, then abruptly he was on solid ground again.

Then as the back of his bound hand felt splinters, Dave knew he was not on solid ground. He was still moving gently up and down on the deck of a ship. Ruefully, he remembered how he had lectured Hodge Twofingers on the ways of crimps. And now Dave had let himself be shanghaied!

He wondered if Twofingers had managed to escape. And if he had, would it do any good? If Seattle police were up to their usual best, any complaining Indian would be ignored. If he persisted, a few days in jail would impress on any benighted savage the error of his ways.

So now what? Dave realized he could disappear for a year

or more on some voyage. By the time he returned his herd, his ranch—even his Indians might be scattered as far as he. And Miss Emily? He strained again, trying to figure out how he was tied. Whoever had done it was an expert. Dave couldn't move. The slightest strain set his head to throbbing so hard he gave up all thought of escape.

"Only two?" It was a querulous old voice. There was a bass rumble that Dave could not understand. "What?" the old man's voice asked. The reply was drowned by the shrill toot of a steam whistle.

Dave lay face up on the splintery deck, staring into a starless, totally black sky. He was overcome by an avalanche of blackness. The next time he opened his eyes there seemed to be less motion to the deck he lay upon. The sky was graying, and he realized abruptly that the long, dark night was over. Staring up at a forest of masts and yards covered with furled square sails, he wondered if day would be any improvement. Gingerly, he tried to move and discovered he was still tied.

Somewhere behind and above him two men were arguing. The bass rumble of one voice was unintelligible, but the querulous old man's replies were loud and clear. "I know it's dangerous," he complained, "but I can't do everything by myself. Where's this goldanged cattle at?"

Cattle! Unbelieving, Dave strained to hear the rumbling reply. The only word he caught was "Georgetown" which, Dave realized, lay halfway between where his herd was pasturing and downtown Seattle. There were too damn many coincidences of late in Dave's life. Could they possibly be talking about *his* cattle? He struggled to focus his eyes. Above him clouds gyrated crazily.

Dave was not a sailor but he had spent his life outdoors. No sky could spin like that. He could see the masts, spars, and furled sails clearly, so he knew it was not his head that was doing the spinning. Sails unset, this ship was moving. It took him a few moments to realize what he was seeing. For a sailing ship to gyrate this wildly, for clouds of coal smoke to drift periodically overhead could mean but one thing. They were being towed up the winding channel of some river by a steam tug.

South, by the coal mine town of Renton, he had driven the herd across the Green River. A ways north of where he had forded, where the river became tidal, its name changed to the Duwamish. He wondered if he was being towed up this river. It would make everything so simple—too simple, he realized. Once already a band of villains had loaded his cattle for him. It couldn't happen twice.

"—leave 'em in plain sight for everybody to see!" the old man's voice was rising.

Moments later somebody tossed Dave over his shoulder like a sack of flour and he felt himself being carried down a ladder where he was dumped in total darkness again. It made no difference whose cattle, he guessed. By the time they got around to untying him Dave knew there would be nothing he could do. He tried to sleep, conserve his strength for whatever opportunity.

At first he thought he was dreaming; then Dave realized he was understanding the faint, husking murmur that came from the darkness.

> "Earth and Air, hear thy child.
> Sun and Moon, hear thy child.
> Snake that eats its tail, hear thy child.
> Spirit of my totem cougar, hear thy child.
> Killer of the Enemy's gods—"

Dave felt a sudden frisson at the realization that he was hearing something no man was meant ever to hear—especially no white man, even if he did happen to understand the old language. And here he had always assumed his Indians were Christian! He tried not to listen as Twofingers continued the chant. He coughed and cleared his throat. Abruptly the soft chanting ended.

There was a long silence. Dave made yawning, stretching sounds as if he were just awakening. "Dave?" It was Two-fingers' voice.

"Yeah," Dave answered dazedly. "Where am I?"

"This child knows not." Twofingers was still speaking the old tongue. "Can that person move?"

"*Heylo,*" Dave said. "And that person?"

Twofingers was squirming and puffing in the darkness. Suddenly Dave caught the smoke and buckskin smell in his nostrils.

"Perhaps if that person could—" Then he felt rope rasp across his face in the darkness. Something struck him across the bridge of his nose, and Dave wondered if his nose would bleed. His eyes stopped tearing and he struggled to collect himself. "That person's hands?"

It was not the easiest thing he had ever done, but Dave realized it might be their only chance. If he and Twofingers could manage to untie themselves before whoever with the rumbling bull voice knew they were free . . . Frantically, Dave began chewing on the ropes.

Working blindly in the darkness, he finally encountered a knot with his lips. He began concentrating on the knot, teasing away with his teeth until finally after half an eternity he felt the manila line begin to slip. After that it was only minutes until Twofingers had freed his hands. Hastily the Indian hitched himself around until he could begin working at Dave's hands.

It cost Dave considerable effort, but he managed to say it. "Perhaps that person's feet first?" he suggested. Twofingers grunted and conceded the wisdom of Dave's suggestion. If they were interrupted before the job was done it might be best to have at least one man totally free.

Down here in the darkness he could hear the gurgle of water slipping past a wooden hull. Topside boots clumped on the deck and there was still the confused gabble of argument. It seemed to Dave as if somebody were stomping on the deck in some irregular pattern, as if trying to send a message. He wondered if there was a captive telegrapher aboard.

Breathing heavily and muttering in a mélange of English and the old language, Twofingers worried away at his feet. Dave knew it was just his impatience, but it seemed to him that his friend was taking longer to get his feet untied than it had taken Dave to chaw beef on the first knots. Still tied hand and foot, he waited to see if Twofingers would make it —and possibly get around to untying him before somebody came down into this hole to check on them.

"Aaaaahhhh!" Twofingers gave a heartfelt sigh and turned once more to begin working at Dave's bound hands. "Ow, ow, ow!" he suddenly moaned.

"That person feels?" Dave asked.

"My goddamn hands!" Twofingers explained. "Sonofabitch tie 'em too tight." Gritting his teeth, he went back to worrying at Dave's bound wrists. Finally he gave up and began chewing as Dave had done.

Overhead the thumping continued along with the one-sided argument. Dave's head was still aching and he supposed there would be a lovely knot on it, but gradually he was becoming aware of the throbbing in his wrists and ankles. Soon he would be enduring the same sensation as Twofingers. Even if they were free it might be days before either of them would be any match for an able-bodied man —even if that man were unarmed. Dave wondered where his rifle was. Probably still in the gelding's saddle boot, he guessed—unless somebody had been able to sweet talk his horse into standing still. He sighed. It might as well be on the moon for all the good it was going to do him here.

Twofingers was still snuffling and grunting as he rooted in the ropes around Dave's wrists. Finally he managed to tease a knot loose. As the rope loosened Dave felt a surge of blood and braced himself for the pain and tingling that would come. Already Twofingers had turned away and was once more struggling with his feet.

"It'll never work that way," Dave said. "You chew on my ankles and I'll see if I can reach yours."

"Come up on deck, you sonsabitches!" It was the rumbling bass voice that had been arguing with the old man.

Dave and Twofingers froze.

"Ain't you got loose yet?" the rumbling voice sneered. There was the sound of a door slamming. Dave wondered if it was bluff. Probably the whoever with the bass voice was just checking.

"This child is having trouble with the knot," Twofingers whispered, once more dropping back into the old language. Dave sighed and hitched himself around on throbbing hands until he could tackle the knots around the Indian's ankles. He began chewing again.

Dave would have been willing to swear no knot could be tied that tight. As a boy growing up in Indian country he had struggled with knots tied in wet buckskin and shrunken dry. How could mere manila be drawn so tight? Strands were caught in his teeth, and he realized dazedly that the warm, salty liquid that drolled from his lips was not saliva. It was blood. Still the knots around Twofingers' ankles resisted him. Grunting and muttering, he teased away at the hemp, pulling it free one strand at a time until finally he felt the bonds loosen. It seemed as if he had been at it all his life, but Dave supposed it hadn't taken over an hour. He wondered if his teeth would ever be the same again.

"This person's feet now hurt," Twofingers growled. He began chewing at Dave's ankles. Dave tried to relax and forget the throbbing pain in his wrists. It hurt so bad he had almost forgotten about his headache.

He put a throbbing hand out in the darkness, knowing it was useless. Whoever had shanghaied him would not be stupid enough to leave anything here that might be used as a weapon.

11

Twofingers still struggled with the knots around Dave's ankles. Dave spread his arms and methodically searched every inch of floor within reach. It was not just empty. The compartment was totally free of dust, as if it had been hosed out. There was not the tiniest fleck of dirt or sand within reach. Dave sighed. The situation was not encouraging. He knew there would be slight chance of surprising their captors. Unless the bass-voiced man was bluffing, he expected them to be free already. Chances were he wouldn't even come down into the compartment after them. He would stand on deck with belaying pin and pistol and, sick, knocked-about as Dave and Twofingers were . . .

Dave struggled to think. His feet were still tied but his hands were free. Twofingers was free. But most important, Dave guessed, his mind was free again, no longer totally blanked by the colossal headache. What had the crimp hit him with? He was putting a hand to the back of his head when he decided it might be wiser not to find out. *Think!*

He couldn't match the shanghaiers with strength. There would be more of them, and they would be armed and in better shape. He and Twofingers couldn't fight it out. He tried to think what a fresh-caught seaman would do—what a shanghaier of a captain would expect him to do?

A man would protest—demand to see proper authorities. A man would waste his breath protesting, struggling, trying to convince somebody it had all been a horrible mistake. A man would wake up and assume he was miles asea already, far from any kind of help. Or . . . a man who knew the sea, had perhaps been shanghaied once before, might attack—which in Dave's weakened condition would only get him another knot on the head, and next time he *would* be miles asea.

Miles asea . . . suddenly Dave knew what had to be done. It was dangerous, might cost them both their lives, but there would be no second chance. Twofingers was still gnawing at his knotted ankles. Dave tried to move his hands. His fingers were swollen from the sudden rush of blood, and his hands felt hot and tingly. He knew he would have no strength to pick at knots. He tried to lay quiet while Twofingers chewed at the knots. Quietly, speaking softly in the old tongue, he explained to Hodge Twofingers what must be done if they were to escape.

"Goddamn knots too tight," Twofingers muttered.

"Come on, you sonsabitches! Up on deck now!" It was the same bull-roaring voice. Dave squinted upward. Total darkness. He decided whoever was just checking—making sure they were still tied and up to no mischief. And the hell of it was, Dave realized, the bass-voiced man was right. As long as his ankles remained tied, he was helpless.

"Christ, my teeth hurt!" Twofingers complained. He sighed, and Dave felt him shift position. He decided the Indian must have given up on the knots. He was starting elsewhere, pulling the rope apart one strand at a time.

Topside Dave could still hear that odd arrhythmic thumping, as if some telegrapher were pounding out arcane messages. The bass voice was once more arguing with the querulous old man. "You want to do it yourself then?" the deep voice growled.

Dave had never been on a ship before, but he remembered the stories one of his father's cowboys had told. According to Sailor Jack, 99 per cent of the time aboard a square-rigger was spent pulling on a rope end somewhere. He listened to scraps of argument and realized that the two voices topside must be the only ones aboard this snugged-down ship. Two against two—which didn't make all that much difference if two were armed and ready and the other two were weak-kneed and still tied up.

And still Twofingers chawed at the rope around his ankles. Dave gritted his teeth, tried to lie still and ignore the throbbing of his swollen fingers. Most of all, he tried to *think*. Irrelevantly, he was reminded of his years-dead father, who had been fond of saying, "People would rather die than think. Somebody proves it every day."

Dave wondered if he was about to prove it. It was a poor plan, conceived in desperation, but it was the best he could do—and he wouldn't even be able to do that unless Twofingers somehow managed to free his ankles.

Finally it happened. Dave felt the bonds loosen as the Indian gnawed through the last strand. There was a sudden rush and tingling as blood began moving through his feet. He braced himself for the pain to come.

Twofingers was sputtering and picking at his teeth. Dave supposed his face would be as bloody as his own. "Can that person stand?" he whispered.

There were sounds of movement, and then Dave sensed that his partner in disaster had made it to his feet. Dave tried and discovered that he could stand too. He wondered whether his feet hurt worse than his head. The compartment was barely high enough for him to stand upright. Twofingers, who was an inch taller than Dave, had already discovered the overhead beams. "That person knows what to do?" Dave insisted.

"This child is ready."

They stood clumsily in the darkness, flexing arms and legs, waiting for the numbness to go away—waiting . . .

Nothing happened. Topside, the quavering old man's voice still wrangled with the bullroarer. By now Dave had pretty well worked it out. There was work to be done—something heavy with a rope. They were needed topside, but both of their captors knew they were too close to shore and civilization. There was a toot from a steam whistle. Abruptly there was a series of toots, and Dave could sense the impatience in the hand that pulled at a whistle lanyard. Topside that berserk telegrapher was still thumping.

There was the sound of a door opening. This time, Dave guessed, it must have opened a little wider, for he saw a hint of grayish daylight, and for the first time he saw the ladder down into this compartment. "On deck!" the deep voice roared. "You think I got all day?"

"Now?" Twofingers muttered.

"Now," Dave agreed. It was his idea. If he had guessed wrong, it would be his head. He started up the ladder.

Expecting a blow at any minute, he put his head cautiously up through the ladder entrance. Topside it was still not fully daylight. Dave could smell the damp, dense-packed fog. He felt Twofingers behind him on the ladder. More slowly and feebly than was actually necessary, Dave crawled out and up on deck. He collapsed, tried to stand, played dying swan while Twofingers made his way on deck.

Finally the pair of them were on deck, standing in sick dejection, twin portraits of misery. Head hanging, Dave struggled to take in as much as he could from the corners of his eyes.

"Up forward. Look alive now!" The bass voice directed them toward a capstan. Dave forced himself to look confused and let the bull-voiced man whack at him with a rope end, herding him toward the bows. The tug had cast off and was somewhere in the fog casting a stink of coal smoke over them. The square-rigger had been joined to a rickety dock by one line. Dave could see now what they were expected to do. The line had to be pulled tight by men walking around the capstan pushing bars. The dock was a hundred feet away and the line was taut, pulled by wind and current.

"Now?" Twofingers murmured as they staggered toward the capstan.

"Now," Dave agreed. Without changing pace they continued to the capstan bars, staggered past them to the rail, and leaned over it to vomit. Leaned far over the rail. Too far. As they fell overboard in the darkness, into fog-covered river, Dave sensed the silent ferocity of a rush behind them. Hands scrabbled at his legs, but it was too late. He heard Twofingers splash, and an instant later his body was assaulted by sudden total immersion in the cold, brackish water of the Duwamish.

Suddenly Dave was wide awake, headache, throbbing hands, and feet forgotten. It had been stupid. Why had he ever done such a crazy thing? If he didn't get up to the surface and get a breath of air he knew he was going to drown before he even discovered which way was up. But if he came up in sight of that ship . . .

He had no idea where he was. Then abruptly his hands felt barnacle-encrusted planking above him. He struggled not to panic. The current was keelhauling him, dragging him along beneath the foul hull. Barnacles tore at him like a hoof rasp, ripping his shirt, ripping shreds of flesh from his back. He struggled to kick himself away, then tried to remember which way the hull had been, keep himself swimming in the same direction.

It was useless to fight this current. He couldn't hold his breath any longer. Now he understood why the line had been so taut—why they had needed a couple of extra hands to winch the venerable hull up to the dock. He wondered if the shanghaiers had already given him up for dead.

Lungs bursting, he let himself come to the surface. He gasped, treading water until he had caught his breath. The fog lay thick over the water. He could not see the ship. Nor could he see anything else except the tiny circle of scummy water in which he floated. Christ, was it ever cold!

Somewhere he caught a whiff of coal smoke, and the tug

tooted again. It was useless. He couldn't tell which way the sound came from. And if he knew, he couldn't keep any kind of a heading. There was a faint breeze across the water. Which way? He didn't know. Dave guessed the only thing to do was try to stay afloat, maybe move a little bit if he could without tiring himself. If he could just keep the breeze on the same side of himself . . . after all, this was a river. There had to be a bank somewhere. But which way? How far?

"Dave?" It was Twofingers' voice.

"Yeah. You all right?"

"Got scraped some, but I'm still afloat. Which way we go?"

Dave searched for the Indian. The low voice sounded less than ten feet away, but he couldn't tell which way. In turning to look for the other man he had lost his orientation with the wind. With the kind of luck he'd been having, Dave knew it was perfectly possible for him to float the length of the river without once seeing a bank. And once he had washed out into the bay . . .

"Where are you?" Twofingers asked. "This child is getting cold."

Dave struggled to calm himself. Relax and float, he told himself. Surely two people this close together couldn't stay lost. But what difference did it make if they drowned together or separately? He didn't need to find Twofingers. He needed to find the shore!

The breeze was whipping up, sending little ripples that threw water into Dave's nose and mouth every time he was less than careful. He kicked and plunged down his arms, drove himself a foot up out of the water for a clean breath of air, and—there was Twofingers less than ten feet away. A foot above water the fog was still thick, but not so hopelessly impenetrable as below. He kicked toward the Indian.

Twofingers was gasping and choking. Dave kept his distance lest the Indian panic and drown them both. "Do it this way," Dave instructed, and showed Twofingers how to kick and force himself upward long enough for a clean breath of air before he sank again.

Only this time when Dave sank vertically under water, his feet struck soft mud bottom. He nearly panicked before he realized he was not permanently stuck. Was it a shoal or were they nearing shore?

"Hey! I touch bottom!" Twofingers was ten feet away and head and shoulders out of the water. Then slowly he began sinking.

"Swim," Dave said. "Don't try to walk." He floundered about until his feet broke free of the clinging mud, and he began swimming past Twofingers. Suddenly Dave's knees and elbows were hitting bottom, only now the mud was firmer. The river, he realized, was tidal, and the tide must be high at the moment. This ooze, at least, was not quite so clinging. Dave slithered carefully through the shallows and heard Twofingers behind him. Finally Dave could stand without sinking.

Dave was mud from head to foot, but he knew better than to try to wash off. He wondered if there would be a firm, sandy beach anywhere. Probably not. This close to salt water there would be only miles of muck. But at least they had escaped the shanghaiers.

Twofingers came to stand shivering beside him. The fog was impenetrable on the water, but at eye level they could see a hundred yards or so—except there was nothing to see. In both directions the riverbank stretched featureless into the fog. If he'd had a coin handy Dave might have flipped it. They turned right and began walking through the grass and ferns that grew rank above the high-water mark. Garter snakes slithered and shore birds occasionally complained. There was no sign of human involvement.

I'm less than five miles from downtown Seattle, Dave told himself. But he might as well be on a different planet. They slogged along through the damp greenery, leaving a trail of mud and trampled ferns behind them. "Maybe we going the wrong way," Twofingers ventured through chattering teeth.

Dave shrugged and continued walking. This couldn't go on forever. Sooner or later they would come to a bridge or a boat landing or someplace where they could get their bearings. They had walked perhaps half a mile already. Dave didn't want to waste time backtracking when help might be only another hundred yards ahead in the fog. Somewhere the steam tug whistled. It seemed practically on top of them. Dave searched for a light or some sign of movement. There was not even a hint of coal smoke this time. He was starting to shiver more violently, teeth chattering beyond all control.

"*Cultus*," Twofingers grunted.

Dave looked down at his feet to see what was bad. He saw tracks. "Well," he sighed, "at least we aren't alone." Then he followed the tracks and saw where they came slithering up out of the tidal ooze. The tracks were his own. Dave had just walked around an island.

12

If Twofingers hadn't been watching, waiting for him to decide what to do next, Dave knew he would have wept. It was just too much. He stood a silent moment, breathing deep, trying not to shiver. Finally he looked straight up and in a grating voice said, "Be advised that on the day I die I may get close enough to get my hands on you."

Twofingers gave him an odd look. "Fork-tongue missionary never teach me that one," he said with a grin. Dave laughed and the moment was over.

"So what the hell we do now?" the Indian asked. "No wood, no matches, and if we build a fire maybe them crimpers come again."

"Crimps," Dave said absently. He tried to think. The island had to be small for them to have walked around it so soon. Now that they had stopped walking, the cold was worse. He turned inland away from where they had slithered up out of the ooze.

As they climbed the dozen feet up from the water's edge they gradually emerged from the low-lying fog. Below them the river and the land were invisible, but above a pearly spot in the sky hinted at sunlight somewhere. In the distance Dave saw the ghostly top of a cantilever framework. He studied the bridge, trying to divine which way the land lay. The wind gusted slightly, and once more they were shivering uncontrollably. It was worse than being in the water. Dave recalled something he had once read about the nature of low-lying fogs—that they were caused when cold air passed over warmer water.

"Look!"

Dave turned to where Twofingers was pointing in the opposite direction of the bridge. Above the fog loomed a small forest of masts and spars, furled sails. The square-rigger seemed practically on top of them. If somebody were to go aloft, Dave and his companion would be clearly visible.

"We gonna freeze," Twofingers managed through chattering teeth. Dave nodded, struggling to integrate a wind direction with current, hoping he was at least on the right river. Was this the Duwamish? If it was then his cattle would be on the south bank, perhaps five or eight miles upstream. Was the current upstream or down? He remembered the high-water marks at the edge of this mudbank island and prayed for some tidal instinct. The wind was blowing toward the bright spot over the bridge. So if the sun was still coming up in the east . . .

He began slogging through the damp grass and ferns down toward the water again. As he stepped back into the river he immediately began to sink into the semiliquid mud. "We goin' back in the water?" Twofingers demanded.

"Warmer in than out," Dave said. He pointed at the faint brightness still visible at this level. "Keep the wind on your left," he said, and threw himself full length into the mud and water. Finally they were free and paddling—Dave sincerely hoped—toward the bridge abutment. Somewhere on the river a steam tug hooted again.

To Dave it seemed a slightly different tone of whistle. He raised his head high from the water to breathe, felt the wind on his cheek, and settled down to swim again. The water was cold, but after strolling about the island in that raw wind it was not as cold as it had seemed the first time they plunged in from the square-rigger. Beside him Twofingers was paddling steadily. For the first time Dave realized they just might get out of this alive. Once they reached the bridge there had to be a road, civilization of some kind. The tug whistled again.

This time it seemed closer. Dave kicked and paddled, forcing his head up through the foot-thick layer of impenetrability on the river surface. He couldn't see the tug, but he could hear the rhythmic hiss-wheeze of a laboring steam engine. It sounded almost on top of them. He wondered if the shanghaiers were out scouring the river for them.

Didn't make sense, he guessed. The old man and bull-voiced duo must have decided they were both drowned by now. The whistle tooted again, and abruptly Dave realized it didn't just sound different. It *was* different. He should have realized there would be more than one tugboat in a busy waterway like this. The tug hooted again, and this time Dave heard a muffled echo. The tugboat pilot was feeling his way up a known stretch of river, stopwatch in hand as he listened for echoes.

There was an abrupt creaking squeal ahead, and Dave knew after a moment's startled thought that the bridge-tender and perhaps his wife were out there walking around capstan bars to swing the low-hung cantilever open.

"Hey!" Twofingers' startled yell ended abruptly as he took on a mouthful of water. Dave turned his head and saw the tug heading straight for them.

"Dive!" he yelled. There was nothing else to do. No time to swim sideways, and this time they would not just drift along the underside of a barnacle-encrusted hull. If the tug's bows didn't do them in, the immense, slow-churning propeller would. He took a hasty half breath and upended himself, clawing frantically for the bottom.

Suddenly the current quickened and he knew he was being drawn toward the screw. Dave struggled frantically, kicking and swimming toward the bottom. Lungs bursting, he struggled to keep his orientation. He was being pulled backward, pulled upward. He didn't know which was up any more. He felt himself tumbling uncontrollably, as if he were inside some gigantic washing machine.

This, he guessed, was it. He felt air leaking from his lungs. If he'd gotten a full breath he might never have been able to dive deep enough. Now, pounded about as he was, he was losing what little air he had. He would never be able to surface again.

Then abruptly he was on the surface, tossed half out of the boiling water. Choking and gasping, he tried to see where the tug was. He caught a vague glimpse of stern, a heavy hawser taut and shedding beads of water. My God, he thought. Now the tow was going to run over him!

A blondish man with a greasy floursack apron around his waist suddenly appeared at the stern. He was tossing a pan of dishwater overboard when abruptly he turned and began yelling something unintelligible.

Dave could hear changing sounds of the engine, and the hawser began to go slack. It would make no difference, he knew. He was barely afloat now, and a tug with a tow was as ponderous, as impossible to stop as an impeachment. He tried to see what kind of a ship—how big?

He could see nothing. There was too much noise from yelling, from engines, from the wake of churned-up bottom mud for him to hear. He wondered if Twofingers would ever appear again. Most probably, pieces of him would appear. Dave wondered how close he had come to the propeller. The wash of that screw was still pushing him away from the slowing tug—straight toward the tow. He had lost all sense of direction. If he tried to swim sideways he might end up lost again. He sighed. He couldn't swim anyhow. It was all he could manage to stay afloat. If only there were a plank or a log—something to hang on to . . .

As if something were reading his mind, a log appeared. Then Dave knew it had appeared much too fast. It was plowing through the water toward him. Now he knew what the tug had been towing: a log boom for one of the sawmills

—which meant he was heading downriver instead of up, as he had thought. Not that it made any difference. Dave had made too many mistakes. This boom could be a hundred feet wide and half a mile long. There was no time to swim to one side. No one had yet invented a way to swim underwater for half a mile. Either he caught that first log and managed to climb atop the boom—or there would be no more choices.

Dave took a deep breath, tried to gauge the distance and speed of the log that moved crossways toward him. He let himself sink, prayed his timing was right, then kicked and clawed wildly toward the surface again. He shot chest-high from the water just as the log came to him, pushing half the river in front of it.

The impact nearly knocked the wind out of him but finally Dave realized it had really happened. He lay half over the log with only his feet still in the water. He hung on, gasping and gagging as he struggled to rid himself of the foul mud.

It took him a moment to realize that the tug had done its cumbersome best to stop once the cook had seen him. He wondered if there would be any chance of finding Twofingers; then abruptly he saw the Indian pulling himself hand over hand along the slack hawser. Moments later the Indian lay gasping and vomiting beside Dave atop the boom. "Christ!," the Indian said between retches, "how'd you like to be a fish?"

The tug was moving again, pulling cautiously. The hawser came from the water, shedding soupy mud as it came taut. Dave guessed the skipper would have his hands full keeping a boom under control in a narrow, winding tidal channel. Then he saw a skiff coming toward them. The boat was empty, drifting stern foremost.

A lot of good it was going to do them, Dave saw. There were no oars in the skiff. How many miles downriver to the sawmill? Possibly not more than four or five. But tugs didn't bother to struggle against the tide. They might anchor somewhere and take a day or two to make those five miles. Meanwhile he and Twofingers could freeze to death. Maybe they'd better get in the skiff and push off past the edge of the boom. Even paddling by hand would beat waiting here to die.

The skiff came closer, still stern foremost, and bumped into the lead log of the tight-chained boom. Dave studied it doubtfully, then saw a rope leading from the bow of the skiff off into the fog. It lay slack in the water, heading the same way as the tautened hawser. Dave shook his head. Maybe it was the cold, but he didn't seem to be thinking too straight. Somebody aboard the tug had the other end of the skiff's painter and was letting it back so they could climb aboard. He motioned the Indian into the skiff.

Twofingers jumped. Dave followed him—straight into another disaster. Whoever was letting out line could not see; he was still letting it out, and the skiff was drifting around sideways against the front of the boom. It was starting to take water over the gunwale. Dave yelled, but knew he would never be heard over the hiss-wheeze of a laboring steam engine. He jerked frantically on the rope. The rope came slowly taut, and the bow of the skiff pulled away from the boom.

Moments later they could see the floursack-aproned man pulling them in toward the low stern of the tug. As he helped them aboard the tug, Dave realized the swim had at least done something for him. He was no longer muddy—just wet.

The cook got them below where galley, fire, and engine rooms were combined. Even as Dave felt the heat sink into him, he found time to wonder what kind of a hell this space must be in hot weather. It was not until Dave and Twofingers sat draped in blankets, their clothes festooned over a steam pipe, that Dave really began to shiver.

As the heat slowly worked into his chilled body, the

shivering became worse, and paradoxically he felt colder, more close to freezing to death.

The blond, walrus-mustached cook made sympathetic noises and handed them cups of soup. Dave struggled to drink his, got a swallow down, and was suddenly nauseated. Hastily, the blond man put a bucket before him. Dave vomited what seemed gallons of muddy water and suddenly felt better. He tried the soup again, and this time it stayed down.

"Don't know how I can ever thank you for—"

The blond man grinned, shrugged, and said, "Yaw."

Dave tried a couple more times before he realized that their rescuer could not speak English.

There was a shrill whistle, then a voice yelled, "Hey, Ole!" There was a spate of something Dave guessed was some Scandinavian language, and after several repetitions he realized that what sounded like "cobble" must mean cable. The cook said "yaw" again and disappeared, presumably to make some adjustment with the towing hawser. Twofingers pulled a blanket snug over his head as he turned to Dave. "Now what we do?" he asked.

Dave didn't know. He finished his soup, and still the cook had not returned. He got to his feet and rearranged their clothing along the steam pipe. Each time he thought he was getting warm, his body would abruptly break into another fit of uncontrollable shivering. He wondered if he would ever feel warm again.

Finally the cheerful cook was down below again, hastily shoveling coal into the firebox. He finished, checked pots on the tiny galley stove, and offered more soup. Dave thanked him and shook his head.

An hour passed and the shivering bouts came farther apart. Finally Dave had to admit that the sweltering galley had brought him as close to normal as he would ever be. He was starting to sweat. He checked his drying clothes.

The tug went into a positive frenzy of whistle blowing

and there were increasingly frequent conferences over the speaking tube. Ole gave them an apologetic glance as he dashed on deck. Dave studied the steam gauge. The needle had swung far in the opposite direction from the red. The next time the cook stuck his head in the galley Dave waved a coal scoop questioningly. "Yaw," the cook said with hurried gratitude. It was not until Dave was heaving coal onto the fire that he realized what all this sudden activity had to mean.

The tug was not anchoring. They must have reached their destination—a sawmill somewhere—and now the tug was nudging the boom out of the river and into a millpond. He wondered where they were. How long would it take to get back to the herd, where he could get another horse from the remuda and resume the search for Miss Emily?

He was still shoveling coal when he heard a noise behind him. "No more," a heavy, aging man said. "We finish soon. What the hell you swim in river for?"

13

"Shanghaied," Dave said.

The tugboat skipper's face lit with comprehension. "Yaw," he said. "Dem sonsabitches almost get my Ole last week."

Dave relaxed. At least he had not fallen into another den of thieves. "Where are we?" he asked.

"Sawmill. Elliott Bay. You go to police?"

Dave shook his head. "Wouldn't do much good, would it?"

The skipper agreed that it would not. "You know who done it?"

Dave wasn't sure. Then, remembering the venomous look of the pair of crimps from whom he had rescued Twofingers, Dave decided he knew where to start.

"You don't got no gun?"

Dave shook his head. He wondered if anyone had managed to shortstop the gelding with his venerable .45-.90 in the saddle boot. Maybe he'd be lucky and the beast would make its way back to camp alone. In the pig's eye, he decided. But he guessed he'd better be philosophical. Being fished out of the middle of the river was enough good luck for a lifetime.

Elliott Bay was Seattle's harbor. They must be within easy walking distance of where he and Twofingers had been bashed in the Pinkertons' side yard. He sighed and resign-edly began putting on his almost-dry clothes.

The aging tugboat skipper was eying him speculatively. "Since every damn fool go chasin' off after gold, dem crimps been stealin' all kinds honest men. You like to fix dem sonsabitches?"

Dave most devoutly would. Twofingers wanted to be in on the fixing. Putting his clothes on, the Indian picked sadly through his pants pockets. "Nothing," he muttered. "'Spe-cially no knife."

"I give you knife," the tugboat man said. He rummaged through a drawer and picked through tools, odds and ends of paperwork, and the sort of things that grow and repro-duce in drawers until he found a knife. Twofingers accepted it with thanks.

The elderly man turned to Dave. "I couldn't give you no gun," he said. "But by yiminy, I got a pistol in that drawer I paid two dollars and fifteen cents for. I'd give two dollars to see somebody put a crimp in dem crimps. You could owe me fifteen cents."

Dave grinned. "I'll pay you back when I can," he prom-ised. "My name's Dave Watkins. What's yours?"

The elderly man held out his hand. "Sven Olsson," he said. "You find me easy in Seattle. Ay bane only Irishman in town wit' a name like dat."

So once more Dave and Twofingers were walking the fog-shrouded streets of Seattle. By the time they had hoofed it from the sawmill back up First Avenue to where they had lost the trail, it was early evening. Dave wondered if the fog would ever lift. More importantly, he wondered what they would find.

Chances were they would find nothing. He hadn't exactly been inside the detective agency's office, so Dave knew he couldn't blame them. The crimps probably had followed him there and waited until he and Twofingers had set them-selves up playing peeping tom at the side window. He would walk into the office and some clerk would smile, shrug, and deny everything. And Dave would be unable to do anything about it because some still small voice would be telling him the clerk might be right.

"There it is," Twofingers said.

Dave studied the small office with the noncommittal sign. Though only a couple of blocks from Skid Road, this street was much quieter. This time of day it was practically deserted.

Twofingers studied the street cautiously before stepping once more over the low fence and into the side yard. Dave stayed in the street. The Indian tried peeping into the window and gave up. Shaking his head, he came back out to the street. Dave studied the door. He could see no light inside, but some dark instinct told him there were people in there behind that curtained door. He put his hand to the knob, and to his surprise it opened.

Inside a man in green eyeshade sat at a desk. Sitting with legs crossed in a chair opposite the desk was a man in Levi's and Stetson. Dave felt he ought to know the man in Levi's, but he couldn't place him.

Later, when he had time to reflect on these events, Dave would ponder the niceties of terms like "guilty knowledge." At the moment things were happening too fast. From the green-eyeshaded clerk's look of surprise and horror it was obvious that Dave would not have to ask who was behind the shanghai attempt.

Twofingers gave a savage growl and sprang. Dave turned on the surprised man in Levi's, suddenly remembering where he had seen that surly face. It was the hip-pocket sheriff in Okanogan—the man who had tried to stop him from moving the herd—presumably the organizer of the posse that had chased the steamboat down the river.

Dave supposed he should have given the man a fair chance, but from the sudden look of surprised recognition he knew the sheriff had recognized him too. Dave came down on top of the Levi's-clad man hard, pounding his fists joyously and repeatedly into a nose that blossomed and bled. It took him some time to realize the other man was no longer fighting back. By the time Dave got control of himself, the sheriff was used up nearly as bad as Dave and Twofingers had been. Dave drew a deep breath and stood.

Twofingers had given the clerk a thick lip and a couple of fat ears and was still lazily cuffing the terrified, green-faced man who had sold him. Dave caught his breath and realized that he was now in even more trouble. One didn't go about beating up sheriffs and Pinkertons with impunity. Suddenly revolted by his lack of self-control, he realized sickly that he had gone too far. Now he would have to silence these men for good.

Or would he? Suddenly Dave recalled why he and Twofingers had come to this office the first time. This sheriff had come clear from Okanogan. Had it been to do the bank's dirty work, or had it been for some other reason even more important to the bank? He remembered while they were driving the herd over the mountains—when old John Whitefeather had played word games trying to learn more about Miss Emily's mysterious past.

Mildly surprised, Dave realized suddenly that the nickel-plated, hammerless .32 the tugboat skipper had given him was still in his pocket. In the sudden explosion of action he had forgotten it. He took it from his pocket now and pointed it at the green-eyeshaded, green-faced man who cowered beneath Twofingers. Pointing the pistol at the clerk, Dave asked, "Where's the girl?"

The man in the green eyeshade would never make a poker player. Instantly Dave knew he was on the right track. He put his thumb to the hammer and realized once again that it was hammerless. The clerk's eyes widened as he saw Dave start squeezing the trigger.

Dave relaxed his pull on the trigger. "Think we ought to torture you a while first," he grunted. Turning to Twofingers he asked, "Should we scalp him or just do the hot pincers thing?"

Twofingers gave Dave an unbelieving look, then understood. "Let me take some skin off him first," he said. "Then we rub in salt."

There was a sudden trickling sound in the death-still office as the clerk relieved himself. Dave raised the pistol again. "If you tell us everything I'll do you a favor," he promised. "I'll kill you quick and clean. Otherwise . . ." He left it dangling.

"Hotel Yesler!" the green-eyeshaded man babbled. "I didn't do nothin'!"

"What name and what room?"

"Her own name." Green eyeshade seemed mildly surprised.

"I've heard several versions," Dave snapped. "What's yours?"

"Emily Jerome, of course. She's in Room 316."

"Why'd you sell us to a couple of crimps?"

Green eyeshade was silent.

Twofingers produced the knife and stroked it lovingly.

"Dollar's a dollar," green eyeshade said sullenly.

So that was that. Dave wondered if the man who sold him had even guessed at any connection between him and the girl. And the girl! So her name was Jerome. Miss Emily was family—probably daughter to the vice president of the North Valley Bank!

This was no time to sort it out, Dave knew. He considered the unconscious sheriff, who would do another man's dirty work for a hundred dollars a month. He considered green eyeshade, who would sell him for less. Neither deserved to live. He ought to kill them—had to, he knew, for after this, if he let them go, neither man would rest until he had killed Dave.

But even as he was thinking these thoughts Dave knew he could not do it. It was one thing to shoot a man in the heat of battle—when that man was trying to shoot one of his Indians. But an execution . . . Bitterly, Dave wished he'd hit the sheriff just a little harder. It was too late now.

What was he going to do? These two were bombs who could go off at any second. How could he silence them?

Twofingers was examining the office. Apart from desk and file cabinets and a windup telephone on the wall, the place was bare. The fire in the potbellied stove was nearly out. The Indian checked the back door. It was bolted. He opened it and peered out into the alley. It was dark—darker than dark now that the sun had faded and the fog had not.

Twofingers closed the door again and opened a file cabinet. Grinning, he pulled out a handful of cuffs and leg irons. Dave reminded himself that this was a Pinkerton agency. He snagged a chair and sat, pointing the pistol at the green-eyeshaded clerk while the Indian shackled and cuffed him. "S'pose they got any keys?" Twofingers asked.

"Who cares?" Dave asked airily. "Just put enough iron on him so he won't float."

It was hard to tell whether the clerk was conscious or not. Dave guessed he had fainted. He stuffed a rag into green eyeshade's mouth and tied it. Then they devoted their attentions to the sheriff, who was just groaning and starting to move. When Dave judged that the Indian could safely finish up he said, "Get 'em out in the alley somewhere and then you hide until I come back."

"*Kumtux*," Twofingers said, which means "understand" in the old language. Hastily Dave exited the front door of the Pinkerton office. He heard Twofingers slide the bolt behind him.

With the pistol buried deep in his pocket, Dave once more began a stroll through the branch office of hell that they call Skid Road. The first bar drew a blank. He put his head through the swinging doors of two more bars before he saw a sleek, dangerous-looking man in low-crowned derby.

The man spun swiftly when Dave tapped his shoulder. The man's hand went toward his pocket.

Abruptly Dave realized it was one of the two men from whom he had repossessed Hodge Twofingers shortly before he and the Indian had both been shanghaied. "Relax," Dave said. "Want to do some business?"

"What kind?"

"Got two ready for delivery."

"Where?"

"How much?"

"Half."

It was a tactical error, but Dave didn't know the price. Besides, he really wasn't doing it for the money. "How much?" he repeated.

The derby-hatted crimp revised his estimate. "I'll give you twenty dollars."

Dave was about to accept when he realized it would never do to be too eager. He shook his head and turned to leave.

"Fifty," the crimp said. "And not a cent more."

Dave nodded and they went down First Avenue, then around into the alley behind the Pinkertons.

Fingering the bills, Dave was torn by conflicting emotions. All his life he had heard about dirty money. Looking at the crisp banknotes, Dave could see no sign of dirt. A streetcar came sparking and groaning along, causing a teamster to get off the wagon and hold his horses.

"Where we goin' now?" Twofingers asked. "Maybe catch that thing and ride out to camp?"

Dave shook his head. Dirty money or not, he had five hungry men depending on him. Fifty dollars could do a lot of things. Someday when he had time for the luxury of a conscience he would do good works and contribute more than fifty dollars to widows and orphans and crippled seamen. But now . . . He looked at Twofingers, whose clothes had not been all that elegant to begin with. After all the mud and river water they were worse. And Dave must look as bad, he realized.

They ranged up Skid Road where an occasional haber-dasher competed with bartenders and painted women for the loggers' and fishermen's money.

Twofingers gave Dave a fishy look. "Why we goin' to spend a lot of money on clothes?" he demanded. "Maybe John and the boys are in trouble. Maybe they're hungry."

"I know they are," Dave said. "But first we're going to visit a fancy hotel, and I want to make sure they don't throw us out."

"Hotel?" Twofingers echoed in outraged tones.

"Hotel Yesler, Room 316," Dave explained.

"Oh!" Twofingers said.

14

By the time Dave and Twofingers' hair had been trimmed within civilized parameters, Skid Road was jumping, as loggers in town from six months away from a woman reached abrupt agreements with women equally avid for six months' pay. Dave walked with his hand on the hammerless pistol in his pocket, with forty dollars and thirty-one cents out of the original fifty jammed down by the barrel of the .32.

"What's the name of that hotel?" Twofingers asked.

"Hotel Yesler." They walked down from First Avenue toward the waterfront and couldn't find the hotel. Dave's new boots were hurting. His feet had had a full day, even without new boots, he guessed. An open-sided cable car came creeping up the hill. They jumped aboard and he had to take the pistol from his pocket to search for fare. The conductor seemed to find nothing unusual in this.

They worked their way around the footboard on the edge of the car until they sat in the front, scanning the street for some sign of the hotel. A half hour later the cable car was turning around at the Lake Washington end of the line. The conductor looked at Dave and Twofingers. "If you're out sightseeing, it's another nickel each to ride back," he warned.

"We're looking for the Hotel Yesler," Dave said.

The conductor shrugged. "Still cost a nickel each," he

said. "Ride back over the hill to Third Avenue, then get off
and walk up two blocks." He hesitated a moment, then
added, "You sure you want to go there?"

"Why not?"

The conductor shrugged. "None of my business," he said.
"But it's a ladies' hotel."

"Oh." Dave tried to hide his sudden heartsickness. So he
had been wrong. Miss Emily had given him still another
surprise. Then he managed to get his feelings straight. If the
girl had taken up residence in such an establishment it had
surely not been her own idea. He remembered the bit of
torn lace stuffed under a rope of old Bolly's packsaddle.
Jennings, Jenkins, Jerome—his instincts couldn't be that
wrong. And whether she had already suffered a fate worse
than death, Dave knew he had to get her out of there
somehow—anyhow!

"Well, you going or staying?"

Dave started from his brown study and found another ten
cents for their ride back over the hill toward Skid Road. A
quarter of an hour later the conductor stopped the car and
pointed. "Two blocks and around the corner to your left,"
he said.

Dave and Twofingers started walking. Within a block the
roistering loggers and seamen had disappeared. The gaslit
street was dim and sinister. Dave gripped the hammerless
.32 in his pocket and walked warily, one eye peeled for
crimps. As they approached the Hotel Yesler he was forced
grudgingly to admit that if Miss Emily had exercised any
choice, she had at least shown good taste. The hotel, he suspected, was going to turn out to be one of those elegant,
New Orleans-style parlor houses he had heard about all his
life but never visited.

The receptionist was a hatchet-faced Carry Nation type.
She looked Dave and Twofingers up and down, and he
guessed he should have spent more money on clothes.

"You wished?" she demanded.

"Miss Emily Jerome, Room 316."

"Wait here. I'll see if she's receiving."

So that's what they call it. Dave debated pushing past the hatchet-faced woman but suspected one shriek from her would produce a platoon of bouncers.

"What kind of place is this?" Twofingers asked suspiciously. Dave didn't answer. They stood while hatchet face tinkled a bell and whispered with the aging vestal in starched apron who appeared. The vestal disappeared up a stairway, and Dave guessed the birdcage elevator was reserved for paying customers.

Minutes passed and the biddy reappeared to whisper to hatchet face. Dave began to wonder. He had always thought a parlor house would be a pleasant place, with a piano and all the things lonely men dream about. This hotel lobby was empty. Were he and Twofingers the only customers? Maybe the price was too high even for a logger with six months' pay . . . He wondered if it might have been better to ask Twofingers to wait outside. Most places in Seattle were a bit chintzy about Indians.

"Miss Jerome is not receiving."

"She's not?"

"You heard me perfectly well the first time," hatchet face snapped.

Dave wanted to ask questions, but the grim woman behind the desk had just implied most emphatically that no questions would be answered. Standing bemused on the sidewalk of the dimly lit street before the hotel, Dave realized his questions had already been answered. If Miss Jerome was not "receiving," it told him several things. He wasn't sure he wanted to know all of them.

So she was calling herself Jerome now. He remembered the self-possessed aplomb that had marked Miss Emily's every action. That assurance came only from having been born with a silver spoon in Miss Emily's lovely mouth—from having been fed with that spoon, pampered all her life, living always with the knowledge that no matter what might go wrong, for a Jerome things could never be that bad. What the name could not avert, the Jerome money could. Miss Emily was a Jerome. Sure as hell she was.

So what was she doing in a parlor house? She hadn't gone there voluntarily. Perhaps wandering the streets of Seattle alone, she had crossed paths with somebody who had never heard of the North Valley Jeromes, who knew nothing of the money behind the name—somebody who saw only a girl in worn clothes on a worn horse—a girl who could be cleaned up and put into a tight-bodiced red dress and . . .

Miss Jerome was not receiving. Which meant either she was still being starved and housebroken—or that she was already entertaining another guest. Dave prayed it would not be the latter.

"What's that funny iron ladder?" Twofingers asked.

"Fire escape," Dave said absently. He studied the Hotel Yesler. There couldn't be three hundred rooms in a building of that size. He studied the three stories and finally reached the obvious conclusion about Room 316. Now why hadn't he ever thought of that before? Because there were no three-story hotels in Conconully, Dave guessed.

"If it's a fire escape why don't it come all the way down to the ground?" Twofingers asked.

"To keep people like you and me from sneaking in," Dave explained.

"Be quite a jump for some old lady," Twofingers mused.

Dave had never paid that much attention to fire escapes. He jumped and missed, getting a painful reminder in the back of his skull as he came down flat-footed on the red brick sidewalk.

Twofingers knelt and folded his hands. Dave stepped in, and this time, with the Indian's boost, he caught the bottom rung. To his surprise the fire escape began swinging down to street level. He guessed he should have looked into it a little better. The aged iron was squeaking like a Catholic in a

Presbyterian hell. A window glowed as someone threw back a curtain.

In a minute the place would be swarming. Dave scrambled up the ladder, Twofingers behind him. They were peering into a third-story window before the folding bottom section returned to its up position with a final shrill complaint.

Dave pushed at the window. It was stuck. He pushed again, and the rain-warped sash finally gave. Three inches up it jammed. Twofingers got his hands in beside Dave's and they heaved mightily. Below them other windows seemed to be opening with no difficulty at all. "Who's there?" a female voice called. For a parlor house it didn't sound particularly seductive.

Groaning and complaining, the sash finally rose high enough for Dave to scoot feet first inside. Twofingers followed, and they found themselves in a corridor. The opened window caused a gas jet hidden somewhere around a corner to flicker.

Somehow Dave had always thought a parlor house would be a jolly place filled with wine, women, and song. This third-floor corridor was positively funereal. A door opened. An aged woman in nightcap stuck her head out, saw Dave and the Indian, said "Oh, dear!," and slammed the door shut again.

Where in hell was Room 316? Squinting, Dave saw 307 over the door whence the old woman had peered. The next door was 306. He spun and bumped into Twofingers. Down the hall another door was opening. They rounded a corner, hot on the trail of 316. Behind them was a shrill crescendo of female voices. "There!" Twofingers muttered.

Dave supposed he ought to knock. But there was no time for formalities. He tried the knob. It turned, but the door refused to open. He stepped back, took two mincing steps, and hit the door with his leg straight out. It burst inward as he and Twofingers plowed into the room.

Miss Emily sat at a table writing. Across from the bed in a ladder-backed rocking chair sat a competent-looking middle-aged woman. She was reaching into a handbag even as she reacted in startled surprise.

"Dave!" There was more than a hint of pleasure in Miss Emily's exclamation. With some tiny, still analytical corner of his mind Dave knew it was the first time she had ever called him anything less formal than Mr. Watkins.

The middle-aged woman's handbag fell to the rag rug, and a Deringer skittered out. With one fluid motion Twofingers scooped it up. He brandished the knife the tugboat skipper had given him and said, "Ugh. Makem nice scalp." He fingered the iron-gray bun, and middle-aged competence evaporated. The woman gasped, showed the whites of her eyes, and fainted.

Dave looked out the room's single window and—no fire escape. He grabbed Miss Emily's hand and they rushed out the door. As they started down the hall, the middle-aged woman emitted a shrill, peanut-whistle scream. It went on and on, and Dave knew she had not fainted. She must have been breathing deep and gathering breath for this prolonged alarum. Doors were open up and down the hall now, and as Dave and Twofingers plowed through the gaggle of women who cringed away at their approach, he realized his accounts of parlor houses must have been somewhat adorned. Most of these women were in their middle years, and the one or two young faces he saw seemed more in tune with sewing machines than with a house of joy.

Several more voices took up the hue and cry. Dave looked around the corner of the corridor, and it was jammed with twittery women in night dress and lace caps. Before him was an elevator shaft but no elevator.

"Stairs," Miss Emily said, and they spun to clatter down three steps at a time. They tore past the hatchet-faced receptionist and out into the street. Behind them the Hotel

Yesler was just blossoming into full cry as heads emerged from windows to shriek "Help, murder, police!"

Abruptly Dave realized his inexpertise in such matters. He guessed he really hadn't expected to find the girl here. If he'd had any real expectations of a rescue he would have prepared better—not let himself be caught flat-footed on a deserted street with a girl and no means of getting away from the shrill voices that seemed to multiply with every shriek. Somewhere in the din he heard the tweet of a policeman's whistle.

"Let's walk south real quiet like," he said. With the girl in the middle, the trio struggled to blend into the scenery. It was not going to be easy, Dave realized, for a white man and an Indian and a young lady in what he suddenly realized was some sort of full-length robe not really suited for street attire to blend into the scenery—especially when they were the only people on this dark, secluded street. Perhaps if they could make it the two blocks to Skid Road they could blend into the roistering mob.

A policeman tore around the corner, trotting with a clumsy gait midway between fat man and dancing bear. "Halt!" he puffed.

Dave and Twofingers froze. He could handle one puffing policeman, Dave knew, but within minutes there might be dozens of them. Already the gasping constable was putting his whistle to his mouth.

"There seems to be a disturbance in that building," Miss Emily said in a glacial voice. "It might be best if you found out whether they're being burned to death or slaughtered in their beds."

The policeman stopped in midwhistle. "Right," he puffed, and once more they were alone. Dave gave the girl a look of unadulterated admiration. Why couldn't he think of clever things like that? Once more the trio strolled toward Skid Road. Behind them the shrieking rose, and Dave found time to wonder if he and Twofingers had been the cause of all that commotion.

They were crossing the intersection a block from Skid Road when Dave heard the groaning hiss of an electric streetcar and saw the obvious solution to how one disappeared quickly in a city. The conductor gave Miss Emily's attire one startled glance before he saw Dave and Twofingers. Face carefully neutral, he accepted their fares.

The car was nearly deserted. It was still foggy, and the motorman had trouble seeing. Clanging the bell constantly, he drove the empty car through a half mile of nothingness.

Dave and Twofingers sat across from Emily, still not quite believing that so many things could happen in so short a time. It had been less than twenty hours since old Bolly had returned to camp with a piece of torn lace jammed under a rope. Dave sighed and wondered how to begin. At the beginning, he guessed. He took a deep breath and said, "Now tell me. Why do you call yourself Jennings or Jenkins, Miss Jerome?"

15

"I'm afraid I don't understand, Mr. Watkins."

"Neither do I," Dave said. "But I've got enough problems without borrowing some high-toned runaway's."

For the first time since he had met her pointing a pistol at Taskoosh in a cabin aboard the *Evalina*, Miss Emily's composure was less than perfect. A moment passed before she could look at Dave. "So you know," she murmured.

"I know I've been harboring the runaway daughter of the man who's been threatening to foreclose on my herd—the man who owns the sheriff in Okanogan County—the man who sent a crew of rustlers to steal my cattle." Dave's self-control was rapidly disappearing. "Who the hell do you think was shooting at us that morning?"

"That wasn't Father." Miss Emily's low voice reminded Dave how high his was rising. The motorman was glancing at them in his mirror.

"It wasn't Santa Claus either," Dave gritted.

Somewhere in the fog a whistle tooted. Dave and Twofingers glanced at each other. Dave was no expert at whistles, but the high-pitched quilling toot seemed very familiar. Suddenly an idea came aborning in Dave's mind. It was half formed, but it was the first hint of a solution to his problems that he had managed to come up with. "Let's go!" he said.

Twofingers seemed infected with the same sense of urgency. They jumped to their feet and waved at the motor-man, who seemed so relieved to see the last of this ill-assorted trio that he did not cavil at stopping right now instead of a half block or a half mile down the track.

The car droned and sparked away into the night, leaving them in fog-shrouded darkness. Dave listened, sniffed, and grasped Miss Emily's hand. They picked their cautious way through the fog, with Dave leading. The night was totally dark without a hint of moon or star, and he was afraid they would step into the millpond before . . .

Then finally there was a light. As he came closer it became a hissing arc light a hundred feet above them. Gradually he became aware of the ghostly outlines of sawmill buildings. To one side of them lay the millpond and on the other side the river. They began walking out the long, narrow wharf to where three tugboats were tied.

Ole still wore a floursack apron when they clumped down onto the deck and into the engine room-galley of the *Fröya*. He sat smoking a corncob pipe in the light of a single case-oil lamp. "Hallo," the blond, walrus-mustached man said cheerfully.

"Is the skipper here?" Dave asked.

Ole smiled but obviously didn't understand. Dave struggled to remember the skipper's name. Finally it came to him. "Sven Olsson?" he asked, struggling to pronounce it as the skipper had.

Ole's face lit up with understanding. "*Minut*," he said and disappeared. Dave heard him clump off along the wharf. Now that the *Fröya* was not working, the banked fires gave out a pleasant warmth on a raw night like this. Dave and Twofingers sat on the edge of a bunk, and Miss Emily sat in the chair Ole had vacated. "Why couldn't it be your father?" Dave asked.

Miss Jerome had collected herself since they began this discussion. "Because, Mr. Watkins, my father has not been in the Okanogan for nearly seven months."

"I got a letter from him."

"You got a letter with his name on the letterhead," Miss Jerome corrected. "A Mr. Skanes has been managing the bank since Father left to raise additional funds."

"Additional funds?" Dave echoed.

"Times have been bad since 1893," Miss Emily said. "Do you think cattle ranchers have a monopoly on suffering?"

Dave had to admit the thought had never occurred to him before. He was about to say something when he heard footsteps clumping down the wharf again. Suddenly nervous, he put his hand in his pocket and fondled the hammerless .32.

But when the footsteps clumped down on deck and into the *Fröya* it was only Ole and his skipper. "Ho! Already you kill dem sonsabitches?" the skipper asked.

Dave shook his head and gave a rapid explanation of what had actually happened. "Wanted to thank you for your help," he said. "And give you back your gun." He hesitated. "But I've lost mine. Can I pay you for it instead?"

"Yah, sure," Olsson said cheerfully.

Dave took a deep breath and continued, feeling his way into the plan that had hatched aboard the streetcar. "Do you own this boat," he asked, "or do you work for the sawmill?"

"Mine," Olsson said. "Vile I keep vum chump ahead of bank."

"Are you free now?"

"You mean if I got a job?"

Dave nodded.

"You got a tow for me?"

"I got a herd of cattle," Dave said. "But I don't have any money."

"So?"

"How long would it take you to get to Alaska?"

Olsson laughed. "How d' hell I know that? What kind of tow?"

"Could you get up steam?"

Olsson glanced at gauges. "Twenty minutes," he said. "But where you go in dis fog?"

"Back where you picked us up."

"Oh hoooo!" The sudden fierce glint in Olsson's blue eyes reminded Dave that not too long ago these blond seafarers had terrorized the world from the Black Sea to Newfoundland.

"Mr. Watkins, just what are you planning?" Emily asked. But Dave was too busy heaving coal into the *Fröya's* firebox to explain.

The needle climbed off the pin on the pressure gauge, and they cast off. There was barely steam to turn the screw, but without a tow and unable to move faster than dead slow in the fog . . . By the time they had finished backing from the dock and were heading gingerly upriver, the gauge had already climbed to twenty pounds. Ole came below momentarily and signaled for Dave to stop shoveling coal. Ole pantomimed and hissed until Dave understood something about the uncontrollable way a coal fire would keep on burning hotter and hotter until the unburdened *Fröya* would be needlessly popping safety valves, wasting water, and muddying up boilers.

Dave left off coaling and went up through the narrow scuttle that led to the foredeck just as the girl was coming back in. "It's cold out there," she said.

It was also dark. Dave stood in the bows looking ahead into nothingness. He could sense the bulk of the huge three-cornered hemp fender that cushioned the bow when pushing, but he could not see the water that hissed and rushed beneath it. He wondered how the skipper managed to orient himself. It must depend on many things, he guessed: a knowledge of tides and currents, a reliable compass, a long marriage between boat and skipper so that the latter could know exactly how long it would take to get from A to B, which in turn required an intimate knowledge of the river.

Which— Dave turned and found his way up into the pilothouse.

Eyes on compass and the second hand of a watch in his hand, Olsson ignored him. Olsson spun the wheel, corrected a couple of times, then carefully wrote the time on a slate before turning to Dave.

"You ever been to Alaska?" Dave asked.

"Yaw."

"I hear there's something called an Inside Passage."

"Yaw."

"What is it?"

Olsson grinned. "You can go outside and it gets bumpy. Maybe you take them over the bows all the way up."

Abruptly Dave sensed that Olsson's comic Scandinavian dialect was something that could be conjured up at will. "So what's the Inside Passage?"

"Most of the way from here you got a coast with small islands," Olsson explained. "You could make it in a rowboat if you took your time and had a little luck sneaking across the open stretches before a blow came up." He glanced at his watch and at the slate before continuing. "But half the time you get weather like this."

"How do you know where you're going?"

Olsson tugged at a lanyard, and the whistle tooted shrilly. He counted the seconds until an echo came back. Once more relaxed, he made a cryptic symbol on the slate and spun the wheel again. "Like that," he explained.

"And you can do that all the way to Alaska?"

"Sometimes. Den sometimes ve tie up and wait for fog to go away. But it takes more than a ship to get your cows to Alaska."

"What else?"

"Vell, your cows—they gotta eat. And the *Fröya*, she eats plenty too. Things is bad here in Seattle. I take a chance wit' you and maybe we make us some money. But unless you got a few hundred dollars to spare we don't get us no coal."

While Dave was considering this, Olsson added, "Also maybe ve get hungry too."

"How long would it take us to get there?"

Olsson shrugged. "You show me vot ve tow and I tell you den."

There was a sudden "different" feel about the *Fröya*. Dave would have been hard put to describe it, but Olsson was suddenly jangling the engine-room telegraph as he spun the wheel. The tug shuddered as the engine reversed and the huge screw began throwing water up under the bows. "Dat was close," he breathed as the tug came motionless and slowly backed off the mudbank. The *Fröya* drifted motionless while Olsson stepped outside the pilothouse to listen and sniff. He went inside, checked his watch, checked the compass, blew the whistle, and counted seconds until three blurry echoes returned. Only then did the tug resume its creeping through the fog.

Dave wondered if it would be like this all the way up the Inside Passage. He went out into the bows again to peer into the fog. There was a faint breeze and it was drifting in patches, occasionally clearing until he could see a hundred feet ahead of the slow-moving tug. Abruptly he saw the dim outlines of masts and spars ahead. At that moment the tug's screw reversed momentarily, then stopped turning at the precise moment to bring the *Fröya* dead in the water. Dave went back into the pilothouse and found Olsson scratching his head as he scrabbled about the binnacle. "What you looking for?" Dave asked.

"Some sonofabitch got to put some iron here," the skipper said. "I never been dat far wrong in my life!"

"Wrong?" Dave echoed. "You hit it right on the nose."

"You loose in the head? That's Crazy Mike's old hulk."

"I don't know whose it is," Dave said, "but I'd swear that's the ship and this is the place we jumped overboard."

"But Crazy Mike's been rotting on the tideflats in West Passage twenty years!"

Dave shrugged. "He was being towed up this river. Must've been planning on going somewhere."

Olsson squinted at Dave. "You get a look? What kind of man is skipper?"

Dave hadn't really seen either man. All he remembered was a bass bullroaring voice that had argued with a querulous old man.

"You got to be wrong," Olsson protested. "Crazy Mike— why would he shanghai somebody? Anyhow, you never see no one wit' a wooden leg now, did you?"

Suddenly Dave remembered the odd rhythmic thumping that had made him wonder if some imprisoned telegrapher had been tapping out messages on the deck overhead.

He explained and Olsson was suddenly laughing. "I be damned!" he chortled. "Crazy Mike goin' somewhere. I never even believe it would float."

The tug's steam engine was practically noiseless at low speed. The *Fröya* ghosted alongside the square-rigger, which was tied with only bow and stern lines to the dock. Dave pointed up at the bow, where bars still protruded from the capstan. There was no mistaking it now. This was the ship he and Twofingers had jumped from. "Could she make it to Alaska?" he whispered.

Olsson shrugged in the dim light of the binnacle lamp. "Maybe. Maybe up the Inside Passage if ve ton't hit no bumpy weather."

Twofingers had found an ax somewhere. He was already climbing up the side of the larger ship. He caught a heaving line the blond, walrus-mustached cook tossed from the *Fröya*'s afterdeck, and moments later he was making the hawser fast around the square-rigger's samson post. The ax thumped as he parted bow and stern lines. Slowly the big ship began drifting away from the dock.

Dave fingered the pistol in his pocket, then climbed up the side of the square-rigger. The tug began a rhythmic hiss-wheeze as it paid out hawser, then the line became taut as the square-rigger's bow began swinging. Suddenly the hiss-wheeze was much louder.

Dave saw a shadowy figure creeping toward him along the open midships deck. Dave was drawing the pistol when he saw it was Twofingers. "Don't scare me like that," Dave muttered.

The Indian put his mouth to Dave's ear. "How many people?" he asked.

Dave didn't know. Slowly they began searching the ship. He wished mightily for a dark lantern. But . . . if wishes were horses he'd be riding his gelding instead of this square-rigger. He wondered if he would ever see his horse or his venerable, octagonal-barreled .45-.90 again. They found a cabin door off the quarterdeck, and as they prized it open Dave could smell the unmistakable odor of an old man living alone. Even before the sound of a match scratching, Dave knew this would be where Crazy Mike lived.

"Who are you?" the querulous old man's voice demanded. "Where we going?"

"Shanghai," Dave said. "Only this time we're taking you."

16

Before the match could go out, Twofingers captured the box and lit another. He screwed up the wick in the gimbaled case-oil lamp and lit it. Dave sat in a chair across from the bunk, aiming his pistol at the white-haired, white-bearded wreck who sat amid moldy blankets. On the deck in front of the bunk lay a peg leg with sweat-grimed straps.

"Who are you?" the old man repeated.

"I'm the United States marshal you tried to shanghai," Dave lied. "At the moment I'm trying to decide whether to take you to a federal prison for hanging or to let my Indian tracker take his own revenge for a broken head."

"I didn't shanghai nobody," Crazy Mike complained.

"You received stolen goods. Don't worry about it. I may take pity on you and let you hang like a man instead of like a skinned-alive snake. Now how many men are there aboard?"

"A hundred!" From the sudden glitter in washed-out eyes Dave understood how Crazy Mike had gotten his name.

"Which means you're all alone." From the old man's deflation Dave knew he was right. Still . . . He found a lantern.

Leaving Twofingers to keep an eye on the old reprobate, Dave searched the ship until he was satisfied they really were alone. He went back into the cabin. "Now who brought us aboard and where were you going?" he demanded.

"I already asked him," Twofingers said. "I don't think he really knows."

"If I knowed I'd tell ye!" the old man said. From the wild-eyed shrillness Dave could guess the alternatives Twofingers had suggested in return for a willful obstinacy. He noticed that Twofingers now held a pistol too. It looked like a Navy Colt. The Indian had a fresh welt across his cheek, but there was also a wisp of white hair snagged in the front sight of the Colt.

"Don't hurt him any more," Dave said. The dirty-old-man smell was suddenly overpowering. Struggling not to vomit, Dave went out on deck. He went to the rail amidships, where the river gurgled only five feet below. Ahead in the fog the *Fröya* was invisible, its presence apparent only in the taut hawser and rhythmic hiss-wheeze of a laboring steam engine.

He looked up and saw a star for an instant before the fog closed in again. The *Fröya's* whistle tooted, and seconds later he heard an echo. Standing alone in the darkness, Dave reviewed his chances. He had created enough disturbance in Seattle for a small army. That woman in Miss Emily's room would probably have some arrangement with the police. With the trail he had left in the Pinkerton office, followed by Miss Emily's disappearance . . . That Okanogan sheriff had been in town. Too many people knew of his whereabouts. Dave could never get away with it. Not with anything as bulky as a herd of cattle to move—not with a rotting hulk that had been on the tideflats for twenty years. Even if he were to scrape up cattle feed, coal, provisions—it was just impossible. But to stay here in Seattle after all the stink he and Twofingers had raised was even more impossible.

Suddenly the wheeze-hiss of the *Fröya's* engine stopped.

There was the sound of chain rattling. The hawser remained taut even as the tug drew near enough for Dave to see it through the fog. It took him a moment to realize that Ole had to be winching in on the hawser, taking advantage of the square-rigger's momentum. Finally the two ships lay separated by less than a dozen feet of hawser. Dave swung hand over hand down to the afterdeck of the tug.

"Tide," Olsson explained. "Ve got him away from de dock —nobody come surprise us now. But we ain't goin' nowhere for four hours until current turns around."

The fog had lifted slightly now, and Dave caught an occasional shadowy glimpse of a willow and rhododendron jungle along the bank. "Which bank am I looking at?" he asked.

Olsson consulted the binnacle. "South."

"Could you row me ashore?"

"Yah, sure."

And so it came about that Dave was slogging along the dirt road that paralleled the south bank of the Duwamish at four in the morning. Even with the lantern Olsson had given him he occasionally stumbled. It took him nearly an hour to regain the site where John Whitefeather and the boys were encamped in an abandoned house. "Herd O.K.?" he demanded of a sleepy Kevin Corcoran.

"Sure, why not? You find Miss Emily?"

Dave stared unbelieving at the boy, slowly realizing that despite all his and Twofingers' adventures they had not been gone long enough for the boys and Whitefeather to become uneasy. "Did my gelding ever come home?"

It was Kevin's turn to stare.

"Better go wake everybody up and tell them to get ready to move the herd as soon's we get a little daylight."

"Sure. Something wrong? You didn't find Miss Emily."

"She's all right," Dave said hurriedly. He left the house and trotted across the road to the general store.

The storekeeper was dubious at first, but when Dave went into detail he became enthusiastic. "Beats haulin' coal to Vancouver. Stick around here and the bank's going to fore-close on me in another week." Suddenly cautious, he added, "It'll have to be quick. They see us and you can guess what'll happen."

Dave knew only too well what would happen if anybody worked out where he and his herd were. "You say the dock's only a mile down the road?"

"South Ninety-sixth Street. I got a wagon but only one horse. Any of yours harness broke?"

Dave guessed old Bolly would do.

John Whitefeather appeared in the doorway. "Bad?" he asked.

"No," Dave reflected. "It might all turn out pretty good if we can just hurry up. Let's start getting that stuff down to the dock."

Whitefeather looked doubtfully at him. "That pile of splinters down the road? By the way, how's Miss Emily?"

"Fine," Dave said absently. *Pile of splinters!* He turned anxiously to the storekeeper. "Will it hold a cow?"

"One at a time maybe."

Suddenly Dave knew it would never work. He had scraped by too many times, left a trail as broad as if he'd been dragging a paintbrush. Surely even the most incompe-tent police force . . . He thought back: Had he really left any trail in the Pinkerton office? Then he remembered the shrieking harridans of the Hotel Yesler. But he couldn't sit here and wait for them to catch up. It would violate the fine old Presbyterian principle of free will. "Let's get a move on!" he yelled and went out to find old Bolly.

"Hey, Dave!" It was young Dan Sinlahekin. "You lose your horse?"

Dave sighed. There was no time for storytelling now. "Why?" he wondered.

"He just come back. Got your rifle in the saddle boot too."
Dave wondered if this might be considered as an omen.

By daylight Dave had unloaded the wagon three times, spacing the loads carefully along the dock's aged timbers. The fog was still there, but with sunlight he could see sometimes for a minute at a time clear across the river. He was clucking old Bolly and the storekeeper's horse into motion for another trip when he heard the rhythmic hiss-wheeze of a steam engine. He waited, then realized it was coming from the wrong direction. The tug appeared, moving with all due deliberation beneath a mushroom cloud of sparks and coal smoke. He saw the log boom behind it and was halfway back to the general store before he realized what it meant. If this strange tug was moving downriver with a boom of logs, the tide had still not turned. The *Fröya* would still be lying at anchor somewhere. He wondered momentarily if the river would be wide enough for this log boom to ease past the square-rigger. He shrugged. If Olsson didn't know his business they might as well find out now.

Whitefeather and the boys had gathered in the strays and had the herd moving toward the dock. The next time Dave returned with a wagonload of feed they were cannibalizing the rail fence of an abandoned nearby farm to funnel cattle onto the dock. Dave studied the groaning structure and prayed. He reflected on the growing hectic quality of his life. He had had the most incredible series of scrapes since boarding the *Evalina* back on the Okanogan. Each time he had come up smelling like a rose. But all it took was one mistake and he could end up irrevocably dead. And even cats only had nine lives. . . .

The next time he came back, the *Fröya* was hiss-wheezing up the Duwamish with the square-rigger in tow. The fog still lay in patches on the river, but Dave knew those bare spars and furled sails could be spotted from miles away. He wondered what had happened to the bass-voiced man who had argued with Crazy Mike while he and Twofingers lay bound in that hosed-out compartment.

It just didn't make sense. Seattle was short of shipping, but why would anyone pull a decrepit old hulk with a decrepit old captain off a mudbank? He recalled the querulous old voice asking, "Where's this goldanged cattle at?" Crazy Mike's nasal New England twang had made it hard to tell if the old man had been saying "cattle" or "candles."

Then Dave was staring in disbelief as the *Fröya* and her tow continued ponderously upriver, ignoring Taskoosh, who whooped and hollered and waved his hat at the end of the dock. The boys galloped along the bank, waving and shrieking as they struggled to get the tug's attention. Finally the rhythmic hiss-wheeze slowed. Tug and square-rigger began drifting backward. Gradually it dawned on Dave that Olsson understood this river and its currents far better than he had imagined. Instead of fussing and huffing for half an hour, he had brought the tow into an eddy that was sending it broadside toward the dock. Moments later Twofingers was tossing mooring lines down to Taskoosh. To Dave's surprise, white-haired old Crazy Mike was on deck too, stumping about under no restraint as he gave totally superfluous orders.

Dave pounded Bolly on the rump and urged the grocer's horse until the driverless wagon was moving back toward the store. He began struggling with the loading chute that Twofingers was rigging beneath a barrage of orders from Crazy Mike. "That ain't no line or lanyard or stay," the Indian finally snapped exasperatedly. "That's *rope!*"

The *Fröya* drifted slowly back to the dock and tied up. Olsson and Ole, still wearing his floursack apron, came off the tug and boarded the square-rigger, where they rigged a sling and began lowering bawling cattle into the hold. The dock was swaying dangerously. "No more!" Dave yelled to Whitefeather. "Keep 'em off until we get these loaded."

Wind and current were conspiring with the square-rigger

until the hulk threatened to push the whole dock over sideways. Dave struggled to get the half-dozen cows up the loading chute. Finally he understood what old Crazy Mike had been chittering about. With derricks properly rigged it was easier and faster to lift the cattle directly from the dock than it was to drive them on deck first. But to lift a cow required half a dozen men on the end of the rope. Dave was wondering if there were a way to get lines out ashore where a horse could tail out on the lift, when he saw Olsson stringing rope in the opposite direction. Once the *Fröya's* steam winch was in operation with Miss Emily in the bows of the square-rigger to relay hand signals, the operation went more smoothly.

The dock was still groaning alarmingly. Dave had half the herd onloaded already. He called a halt and they concentrated on loading the storekeeper's cattle feed and other supplies. If the dock collapsed at least Dave wouldn't be totally unprepared.

The dock had been emptied of supplies and they were once more loading cattle when the storekeeper reappeared with the wagon. Dave's legs were trembling and the lump on the back of his head was starting to throb again. The others were as exhausted as he. He wanted to call a halt and catch his breath, but there would be time for that once they were loaded and under way.

Rigging the sling beneath still another bawling steer, he wondered what he was going to do with Miss Emily. Then he remembered he still had nearly forty dollars in his pocket from the sale of the Pinkerton and the Okanogan sheriff. That ought to be sufficient for a spoiled runaway to get back to her folks. By now he suspected the girl would have learned her lesson.

He glanced toward the bow, and the girl was gone. Young Dan stood in the narrow vee ahead of the capstan relaying the hand signals Olsson was giving from the edge of the midships hatch. Now what? Dave wondered.

His questions were answered fifteen minutes later when the girl emerged from the *Fröya* bearing a huge tray of sandwiches and a coffee pot. By unspoken agreement everyone stopped work and began eating breakfast. While Dave gulped coffee, another tug with a boom of logs came creeping downriver. The whistle tooted, and downriver somewhere in the mists of the now scanty fog another whistle answered. The boom of logs sent a long wave toward the dock, and suddenly the tug and square-rigger were conspiring to push the rickety structure over. Dave held his breath.

He was close to exhaustion. Squinting ashore where Whitefeather and Kevin Corcoran held the remainder of the herd, he guessed they were three quarters loaded. If only the dock held out long enough. He would have to work slowly, not let more than one cow at a time onto the rickety structure.

Miss Emily came back collecting empty coffee cups. She bore his octagonal-barreled .45-.90. "Mr. Watkins," she asked, "could you lend me your pistol?"

"Why yes, I guess so," Dave said. "You expectin' trouble?"

The girl pointed. Coming upriver was a steam launch filled with men. In the bow stood a man with field glasses, watery sunlight glinting from the lenses as he studied the activity aboard the square-rigger.

17

Dave stared back. He had heard of sodbusters back in the prairie states praying for rain. He wondered if anyone ever prayed for fog.

As if in answer to his prayer, the watery sunlight disappeared behind a cloud, but before there was time for Dave to become a True Believer the miracle petered out. The weather was cloudy again, but the fog had turned into a faint haze. He could see the opposite bank of the Duwamish. He could see a mile up and down the river. Most of all, he could see the glint of gun barrels among the tightly packed men aboard the steam launch.

John Whitefeather had come up onto the dock, leaving young Kevin to manage the few cows still ashore. For once the older man did not say "Bad?" Staring dubiously as the steam launch wheezed up the river past the dock he muttered, "Hunt ducks. They don't come for us."

"Yeah," Dave said dispiritedly. He remembered how he had hidden in a horseshoe bend of the Okanogan, waiting for somebody else to load his cattle aboard the *Evalina*. Now, he strongly suspected, somebody was going to return the compliment. He watched while the steam launch puffed upriver. Not a single man aboard the small boat looked back, not even the man with the field glasses.

"Send 'em up one at a time," he told Whitefeather. The Indian nodded, and Dave knew neither of them believed this was any boatload of duck hunters. He wondered if the police—surely any city this large would have its own police boats clearly marked. Was it some private army? Pinkertons? There were so many possibilities. Had the Okanogan sheriff known he was here? The information might have been pried out of Miss Emily. She might not have considered it important until it was too late. It might even be some other bank, Dave realized. Maybe whoever held the paper on the slight-statured storekeeper who was driving up with a final load of supplies . . .

They plunged into a renewed frenzy of loading. When there were less than a dozen cows left, Dave came on deck where Olsson superintended lowering the bawling beasts into the hold. "Did you see that launch?" Dave asked.

"Yaw."

"How soon can we get moving?"

Olsson signaled, and the cow was lifted into the air. He signaled again and the terrified critter descended into the hold. The tugboat skipper glanced at the high-water mark along the riverbank. He consulted his watch. "You get everyt'ing aboard in a half hour," he promised, "we make it downriver and into the Sound before the tide changes."

"Yeah?" Dave asked. "Can we outrun them?"

Olsson gave him a pitying glance. "Tide work for us, it work for dem too."

Dave sighed. He wondered what he could do. Twofingers had Crazy Mike's Navy Colt. Miss Emily had Olsson's hammerless .32. Dave had his .45-.90 back. The steam launch held at least a dozen men, each with a rifle or shotgun of some kind. He remembered the perky way that little launch had breasted tide and current upriver. There would be no contest in catching up with the *Fröya* as she dragged this mass of barnacles downriver.

Finally the last cow was aboard. The storekeeper had stripped his stock. He came aboard. "I ain't stayin' behind to face the music," he explained. "Besides, you'n me didn't exactly grow up together."

Dave could see the man's point. It made little difference. If hauling cattle at sea was the nightmare of prodding seasick critters onto their feet lest they lie down and die that Sailor Jack had always said it was, another hand would be welcome enough. He was more worried about Miss Emily. Perhaps there would be a quiet port up the coast somewhere and the girl could make connections with something eastbound. Then he remembered she wasn't really from Providence or wherever she had claimed. Miss Emily was from the Okanogan. They cast off lines, and the *Fröya* paid out hawser. Slowly, the high-bowed square-rigger swung away from the dock. Its stern gave a final bash, and the last twenty feet of dock collapsed with a watery sigh. Dave tried to count his blessings, but as the square-rigger headed downriver he glanced astern and saw the steam launch. It had been hiding, he guessed, around the bend upriver and just out of sight. Now it was following them downriver.

He glanced at the sky. It was cloudy, but to the west the late-afternoon sun came brilliant through an opening. The tug and its tow were silhouetted mercilessly. Dave looked back, wondering how long till nightfall. Even in this lawless city he guessed a private army of pirates might hesitate to attack as long as there were too many witnesses. A while ago he had been praying for fog. Now Dave wished it were earlier in the day, that the sunlight might last for hours yet. How long would it take for the *Fröya* to drag this barnacled hulk out somewhere too exposed for an overloaded steam launch?

Dave was vague about the geography here. Seattle fronted on Elliott Bay, which was part of Puget Sound, which was an immense bottle loosely corked by Vancouver Island. But apart from his single involuntary and largely unconscious trip from Elliott Bay around and up the Duwamish, Dave had never even seen the Sound.

What would happen when the band of ruffians in the steam launch attacked? Either way Dave would have to divide his forces and his limited firepower. If they took the steam tug he was helpless. If he put all his people and all his guns aboard the tug the pirates could board the square-rigger and cut loose, leaving him in a hole with no ace.

The *Fröya* was two hundred yards away at the other end of the hawser anyway, so it was too late now. He was on the square-rigger with Whitefeather and the boys, Taskoosh and Twofingers were aboard the tug along with Miss Emily, which meant there were two pistols aboard the smaller vessel and he had his .45-.90 back here. It was about even, he guessed.

He considered the sun. As often happens about sundown, the western sky was clear even though everywhere else was covered with clouds. It would take an hour for the sun to go down, another half hour or so before it grew dark enough for the men in the steam launch to make their move.

"Pirates, hey?" Startled, Dave turned to see Crazy Mike at his elbow.

"Coulda told ye," the old man cackled.

Dave sighed. He had forgotten about the old man, who had hovered on the fringes of their cattle loading, giving incomprehensible orders in a nautical jargon no cowman could be expected to understand. He supposed he'd have to lock this peg-legged wreck in his cabin before he dreamed up some deviltry or caught a stray bullet. "What could you have told me?" he asked.

"Skanes ain't lettin' you get away with old *Emily*."

"Old?" Dave was startled.

"Sixty-five years this spring."

Dave stared. He shrugged. No wonder they called him Crazy Mike. "Who's Skanes?"

It was Crazy Mike's turn to be startled. Turning washed-out blue eyes to Dave, he gave a wild giggle. "Y'll find out soon enough—once that steam launch catches up."

Something tinkled dimly in Dave's memory. *Skanes.* Where had he heard that name before? It wasn't the sort of name you ran across every day. "What makes you think Miss Emily's an old lady?" he probed.

"Sound as the day she was launched," Crazy Mike cackled. "But I was only a tad o' ten when she went down the Clyde back in eighteen and thirty-two."

Dave stared. "You're talkin' about this ship," he finally managed.

"You crazy?" Crazy Mike asked. "What else would I be talkin' about?" Without pause the old man shifted subjects. "Now, the last time I had t' repel boarders—that 'uz in the Sulu Sea back in sixty-eight." He subsided into a studious silence. "'Course, them Malay pirates didn't have much in the way o' guns."

Dave studied the steam launch, which lazed along just beyond accurate rifle range. He wondered if the men aboard knew he had a rifle.

"Way to handle boarders," Crazy Mike was saying, "is git up in the top hamper with a good cheroot and a few half sticks o' dynamite on a two-second fuse."

Suddenly Dave was listening. "You've got dynamite and fuse?" he demanded.

"No dynamite," Crazy Mike said sadly. "Ain't had none for years."

"Another good idea blown to hell," Dave growled. He turned to squint into the sunset. There was a tiny hummock of grass in the midst of a mudbank, and he realized with a start that this must be the island he and Twofingers had circumambulated in the fog. "What's that dock over there?" Dave asked, pointing upstream opposite the island.

"Coaling dock. Now, if them boarders was barefoot savages, we could sprinkle carpet tacks on deck."

"How far are we from the mouth of the river?" Dave demanded.

"We might rig antiboarding nets amidships," Crazy Mike said doubtfully.

"How far?" Dave repeated.

"Little under three miles."

"Will we make it before dark?"

Crazy Mike squinted watery blue eyes at the water that swished past. "Not even if we had the spring tide," he said.

Dave sighed. Not that it made any real difference.

The fog had lifted and the wind was almost dead calm, he realized, as he studied straight-rising smoke from the launch behind and the *Fröya* almost an equal distance ahead. He wondered why the tug had to let out so much hawser between the ships. Something to do with the wash from the screw?

Studying the *Fröya*'s foamy wake, he guessed the tug's tremendous slow-turning screw must churn up a lot of water. Probably a tow moved better if that backward-moving slug of water was given a chance to quiet down. "How fast are we moving?" he asked.

"Maybe five." Crazy Mike paused. "Hard tellin' with these currents. Git up there to the narrows by Idaho Street and ye may not move at all."

"Unless the tide's right?"

"Unless the tide's right," the old man echoed.

Mike studied the steam launch, which kept its distance. It was a pointless question. They would never be allowed to escape from this river. But he might as well make conversation with this demented old coot. "How fast could we move out in the open sea?"

"Ye might make ten if the wind and the current's right," Mike answered, "but I wouldn't count on better'n four."

"Current?" Dave asked. "You got currents out in the open sea?"

The old man gave him a pitying look.

"I suppose you know all about feeding cattle!" Dave snapped.

"Half ton a head a month if you want no weight loss. Ye'll git by with less if you feed mill shorts."

Dave stared, wishing he'd kept his mouth shut. This old man must have skippered cattle boats in his day. He was chastened with this reminder that even crazy old men sometimes know more than their juniors. But how crazy was this watery-eyed peg-legged wreck? "How come you ain't raisin' a fuss?" Dave asked.

Crazy Mike gave him a shrewd look. "Me'n *Emily* been on the beach nigh onto twenty years. We don't care that much who or what we haul—long's we're finally goin' somewhere again."

Dave wondered if someday he would be that old, that bored with a life that had passed him by—that desperate for any kind of action. "Is that why you shanghaied me?"

"I didn't shanghai nobody, boy. That 'uz Skanes' doin'. Come by a couple o' days ago and said he'd found me a crew and a load o' cannel."

"Didn't he tell you they weren't his cattle?" Dave demanded.

"Not cattle, boy. *Cannel.*"

Dave stared. "Candles?"

"Don't know much, do you, boy?"

Dave guessed he didn't.

Crazy Mike gestured back at the dock Dave had asked about. "That's the coaling dock," he repeated. "I was tied up there to take on a cargo of cannel until you an' that Indian came along."

"I still don't know what cannel is," Dave complained.

"Cannel coal, boy. The kind that burns hot and bright and makes all them sparks you're lookin' at out o' the funnel o' your towboat—and that launch back there."

"Oh." Dave sighed and squinted into the sun again. It had dropped halfway since the first time he looked at it. He squinted downriver past the *Fröya*, but the channel wound on farther than he could see. A mile ahead there seemed to be a sharp turn.

"Harbor Island," the old man said to his unasked question. "If your towboat skipper's got his head screwed on right he'll take the West Waterway."

"Why?"

"Shorter, a little wider, and not so much traffic. Be up there where he makes his turn," Crazy Mike continued. "When he has to sheer off and lose headway turnin'. That's when they'll attack."

Dave looked behind. Was he imagining it or was the launch full of hired killers pulling closer?

18

Dave wracked his brains. This peg-legged old man was a
gold mine of useless information. If only he could come up
with some practical advice . . . "You said something about
nets to repel boarders," Dave pressed.

"But if they see nets here they'll just go on and take the
towboat instead," Crazy Mike said.

And kill Miss Emily!

He sensed a change in the movement of the ship and
wondered if they were at the bend around the island already. Then he saw the tug slightly closer. It took him a moment to realize Ole was winching in the hawser to shorten
the distance between tug and tow, which slowed down the
towing operation even as it gave greater maneuverability
around tight curves. The steam launch behind them was
under no such restrictions. Belching a Roman candle of
sparks from cannel—coal, the launch was within rifle shot
now. Dave wondered what would happen if he put a shot
into the launch. It lay low in the water, showing only the
bows throwing up foam, and amidships a vertical boiler and
a stack that extended through the canvas canopy. He considered the distance. What would happen if he were to put
a bullet through that boiler?

"Spout a lot of steam and maybe scald somebody," Crazy
Mike said. Dave wondered if this watery-eyed wreck was a
mind reader. "But they'd make it ashore and then when a

bunch of innocent hunters complained, you'd have half a dozen police boats out here t' sort out things." He cocked a watery eye at Dave. "Might be some question of who's shanghaiin' who," he cackled.

Dave stared at the old man. "Which side're you on?" he demanded.

"I'm on Crazy Mike's side. Oh, yes, I know what they call me. Man gits old, he has to take care o' hisself." He cackled again and did a hornpipe step with his peg leg. "Sixty years asea and see what it gits you. Don't ever go for a sailor, boy."

Dave hadn't been planning on it. "All right," he said. "You don't seem to care any more for them than for me. Will you help us beat them off?"

"Been tryin' t' tell you all the time, boy. That Skanes is just plumb bad."

Dave could see how it was. An old man down on his luck . . . What would the police of this wide-open town do to protect some poor old man with a sobriquet like Crazy Mike? "They treat you rough?" he asked.

"Ain't as strong as I once was, boy. Old man has t' look out for the main chance."

Dave wondered. With a dozen armed men drawing near, he didn't think that much of his chances.

"Coal barge!" Crazy Mike was muttering. "Cut poor old *Emily*'s masts off! You wouldn't treat a lady like that now, would you, boy?"

Suddenly and for no reason, Dave found tears in his eyes. "No, Captain," he admitted. "I don't think I could do that."

He pulled himself together. Now was no time to get sentimental about some broken-down old man and his broken-down old ship. The steam launch was closer, and he could see the long, low outline of the narrow hull, punctuated with a high stack rising amidships through the canopy. He rummaged about the deck where ropes and slings had not yet been put away. He was picking through the ropes for a suitable piece when he realized his saddle and lariat lay alongside the aftercabin scuttle, along with his .45-.90. He got the lariat and uncoiled it.

He wondered what the people aboard the *Fröya* were doing in preparation. The tug was lower in the water and would be easier for these pirates to board. He glanced forward, and the tug was much closer now. He could see Ole, still in his eternal floursack apron, manning the winch, while Dan and Kevin struggled to coil the hawser. Miss Emily was nowhere in sight.

Dave formed a loop and spun it. His rope had been coiled too long in this damp climate. He studied the approaching launch and guessed there might be time. He fastened one end of his lariat to what a seafaring man would know as a tops'l halliard, and the other about a belaying pin. Hauling mightily, he stretched it. After a preliminary snake dance the lariat lay on deck this time and coiled flat. He tried to spin a loop again with better luck. Crazy Mike watched without comment.

The launch was within a hundred feet now, slowly gaining on the *Emily*. Dave glanced ahead. Ole had winched the hawser up until the tug was within a hundred yards. It was turning already. Dave felt the slight vibration as the *Emily*'s bow was pulled to one side. Suddenly Crazy Mike was stumping off toward the whaleback wheelhouse on the quarterdeck. He struggled feebly with steering gear that had been twenty years on the mudflats, and he finally managed to turn the wheel. Dave guessed he was helping the aged square-rigger make the turn into the narrow channel past the island.

Dave could hear voices on the launch now, though he couldn't understand the words. One voice was very like the basso profundo rumble that had participated in his and Twofingers' shanghaiing. The tall funnel was suddenly belching twice as many sparks as fresh coal was tossed into the firebox. Dave could hear the hissing roar. The launch began moving faster. He checked his .45-.90. He checked his lariat. He wondered if they would begin shooting.

They'd better. If they didn't and if he were to open fire, they would be able to claim innocence and return with a small navy of harbor police. The launch was coming up fast on the starboard quarter, though Dave would have said it was catching up from the right. It drew alongside less than a dozen feet from the low midships section of the *Emily,* and Dave waited with lariat and Winchester to see if they would try to board. Suddenly he realized they were not going to try to climb up the side toward a man with a rifle firing down. Heading for easier pickings, the steam launch was heading for the *Fröya.* Dave put down his .45-.90 and spun his lariat.

It was tricky to toss down from this angle. All his life Dave had been tossing loops at horses in corrals, at calves, and an occasional ailing steer. But to his satisfaction, he saw the oversized loop settle neatly over the spouting smoke-stack that projected through the canvas canopy. Hastily, he dogged the other end of his lariat at the pin rail.

As the line came taut there was a rusty shriek of complaining metal. Dave had been hoping he might capsize the narrow-hulled, overloaded launch—or at least tilt it enough to take on water and embarrass the occupants.

Instead, the funnel tore off with a final scream and popping of rivets. Smoke and sparks boiled up under the canopy, and the crowded men beneath were suddenly choking, gasping, and cursing as they struggled to scoop hatsful of water and drench the canvas. Knives flashed and for moments it was touch and go, but finally the canopy had been cleared from around the stump of stack. Dragging great festoons of smoldering canvas, the launch continued on toward the *Fröya.* The men behind the engine were batting at sparks, gasping and coughing, but the steam launch was still moving—faster than ever, it seemed to Dave. He wondered if he might not more profitably have spent his time killing two or three.

Squinting into the setting sun, he tried to connect up a body with that deep, booming voice. Skanes—whoever Skanes was—had to be the man who had shanghaied Dave and Twofingers, who had come up with some scheme to haul coal. To Vancouver? Coal to Vancouver seemed to be local dialect for coals to Newcastle. Dave supposed the Canadian city must be endowed with ample supplies of its own.

The *Fröya* stopped pulling and, being smaller, lost way much faster than did the barnacle-encrusted *Emily*. As they drifted toward one another with the launch in between, Dave hoped for one happy moment that the spark-belching launch might be crushed between them. But whoever was piloting the launch had his head screwed on right. As the *Fröya* came dead in the water and began swinging broadside toward the *Emily*, the launch hastily sheered off to hold position by the tug's stern.

The *Fröya* had been built for towing and hence its stern was low, less than a foot above the waterline. Between the stern's towing bollard and winch was a pile of figure-eight-coiled hawser. The hempen hawser was six inches thick, and its tough flexibility would stop a small cannonball. Still, Dave was not happy at the thought of his men—of Miss Emily—crouching behind it waiting for the first shot.

Would these ruffians board without shooting? Maybe they would. Dave guessed they might be as aware as he of how close both sides in this affair were skating to the edge of the law. No man in his right mind welcomed a murder charge. But twelve men with rifles and shotguns in an overloaded launch in a narrow channel at sundown . . . could they be in their right minds?

The *Fröya* was still swinging, and as Dave saw the sudden boils of water beneath the tug's stern he realized Olsson was not exactly drifting. He was pulling off some compli-

cated footwork with screw and rudder until the tug was
turned with its bow toward the deepest part of the channel.
Behind the tug, the steam launch still jockeyed for position
in the hundred-foot space between the tug's stern and the
half-mile-wide shore of low-lying mudflat.

Why, Dave wondered, didn't Olsson cut loose, spin about,
and try to ram them? But he knew. For the *Fröya* to outturn
this launch was as unlikely as an ox team outmaneuvering a
quarter horse.

Slowly, the *Fröya* stopped turning. She lay dead in the
water like a sacrificial lamb. Dave supposed Twofingers and
Miss Emily would be crouched behind the pile of coiled
hawser, taking aim with their ill-assorted pistols—as if a .32
could hit anything farther than the width of a brothel bed.

There was a sudden Scandinavian shout aboard the
Fröya, a jangling of bells, and a toot of whistle. Abruptly
white water boiled around the stern of the tug as the tremendous screw attempted to dissipate the energy of full
speed. The tug was motionless. Something had to give. It
was the river behind the tug that gave—great gouts of slime
and mud torn from the shallow bottom to boil up in the
frothing foam that suddenly surrounded the steam launch.
Water spilled over the launch, went down the hole where
the funnel had been, and there was a sudden whump-
whoosh of erupting steam and cinders. The river behind the
tug's stern was covered momentarily with a cloud of steam.

When it cleared Dave saw the launch bottom up, its tiny
propeller still slowly turning. Around it hats floated. Men
floundered, gagged, and cursed as they wade-swam toward
the shore. Dave remembered his own adventures in that
ooze, which seemed perversely to pull any man deeper the
harder he struggled. He noted with grim satisfaction that
not one of the struggling men held a gun.

The *Fröya* had throttled down already and was turning,
maneuvering carefully to keep the hawser out of its screw.
Moments later the *Emily* had straightened out and was

moving sedately down the West Waterway toward Elliott Bay.

Crazy Mike was smiling. "That towhead towboat man of yours is a smart young feller," he said. "I ain't seen that trick since once in Singapore."

"How far is it to Alaska?" Dave asked.

"Seattle to Skagway?"

Dave didn't know.

"I s'pose you're plannin' on takin' them cows to the Klondike where they's gold, ain't you?"

Dave hadn't really been planning on it, but since he had worn out his welcome in Seattle . . .

"Skagway's as near as ye'll git to the Klondike by water," Crazy Mike explained. "Little under twelve hundred miles." While Dave was struggling mentally to divide four knots and twenty-four hours into twelve hundred miles the old man added, "Twelve days, if ye don't have to sit out a blow alee some island."

"And if we don't sink."

"The *Emily's* sound as the day she was launched," Crazy Mike bristled.

"And so are you." Dave struggled to put sincerity into it, but the old man turned to face him.

"They call me Crazy Mike," he said in his querulous old voice. "Ain't nobody ever called me stupid."

Dave had no answer. He looked ahead toward the *Fröya*. Somebody was climbing into the skiff that had been let down once more over the stern. Dave couldn't tell who. It was getting dark now, and he could barely make out the flash of white that was Ole's floursack apron as the cook-fireman-engineer paid out line to let the skiff fall back toward the *Emily*.

The skiff came closer and still Dave could not recognize the figure in dungarees and watch cap. The skiff was bumping alongside the *Emily* and he was stretching a hand to help the stranger aboard before he realized it was another

Emily, this one considerably less than sixty-five years old. "Accommodation is cramped, Mr. Watkins," she explained. "I thought there might be more room here."

Dave was flabbergasted. He had never seen a woman in man's clothing before. The girl saw his discomfiture. "Surely you didn't expect me to travel all the way to Alaska in a dressing gown," she said.

"I hadn't thought about it," Dave admitted.

"That's understandable, Mr. Watkins," the girl said gravely. "And I hesitate to trouble you any more, but Mr. Olsson wished me to convey that he has coal for a half hour's steaming."

Dave stared. In the rush to get cattle and feed aboard he had completely forgotten about the *Fröya*'s needs. Now just where was he going to get a few tons of coal?

19

The girl stared at his sudden discomfiture. "Is something wrong?" she asked.

Crazy Mike appeared out of the darkness from some mysterious errand. Absently, Dave noted that the skiff was being reeled in again. The ancient peg-legged skipper tossed a bundle at Dave's feet and kicked it with his peg leg. The bundle unrolled and became a half-dozen black canvas bags with tumplines and shoulder straps. Though black, Dave could see that the canvas had once been white.

"Mr. Olsson seemed to think there would be coal aboard this ship," the girl said.

"'Course they's coal here. Didn't I tell you I 'uz at the coaling dock for a cargo o' cannel, boy?"

Dave was dazed. "Coal to Vancouver," Crazy Mike cackled. "Only this time 'twas no joke. Them Canadians are all on strike and they ain't a stick o' wood in town to git anybody through the winter."

"Strike?" Dave echoed.

"Sawmills, shingle weavers—whole danged lot! Skanes is a bad one, but he can smell a dollar eight points off the wind."

"You've got some on board?"

"Had one bunker half filled when they knocked off for the night. Woulda had more if you and that Indian hadn't been so bright and early."

Vaguely Dave remembered driving his herd past the coal

mine upriver at Renton. He should have guessed. "Is it enough to get us to Alaska?"

"Ought to be," Crazy Mike opined. "But you shoulda listened t' me this mornin'."

Dave remembered when they had begun loading cattle and the old man had chittered about offering a constant stream of unwanted advice. A lot of good it did him now to realize that, though this peg-legged and rheumy-eyed man might be ancient, he seemed far from crazy. "What else did I do wrong?" Dave asked.

"Ye'll have to shift cargo," the old man cackled. "Ye got cows on top o' the coal!"

There was a bump alongside the *Emily;* then the boys' broad, dark faces appeared amidships. Dan and Kevin clambered over the rail. "Where's the coal?"

Dave was bone weary, ready to drop. He wondered fleetingly if they couldn't just anchor somewhere until morning. Then he realized they were still in sight of Seattle—just exiting the Duwamish into Elliott Bay. Overhead the clouds were socked in solid, but to his right he could see the lights of piers and docks. The waterfront was less than a mile away.

He held a lantern over the still-open hatch and studied the tightly packed cattle below. "I don't see no coal," he protested.

"'Course not," Crazy Mike cackled. "Ye'll have to pull some stanchion boards and move the cattle into another bay so ye can lift the floorboards. Cannel's down below."

There was a deep-throated whistle, and moments later Dave saw a huge boat festooned with lights passing astern. "What was that?" he breathed.

"Bremerton ferry," the old man snapped. "This ain't no place to hang around just makin' steerageway."

Dave suddenly understood why the sound of the *Emily's* passage was muted. Olsson was saving his coal as long as he could. They scrambled below and dodged horns, struggling to lift boards from stanchion grooves and prod crowded cattle into even greater togetherness. Finally floorboards were up and they could drop down into the next section of hold. Dave took the shovel the old man dropped him and filled a sack. He passed it to Kevin, who got his arms in the straps and climbed the eighteen feet to the deck. Moments later the skiff was being pulled back up to the *Fröya*. Before it had been let out to bump once more against the side of the larger vessel, Dave could feel and hear the increase in speed as the tug went into forced draft.

He found himself doing mental sums, trying to calculate how many bags of coal it would take to get the *Fröya* through the night—how long until he could lie down and sleep. But even though he was no sailor, Dave knew the rest of the twelve hundred miles to Skagway might not be as glassy smooth as lower Elliott Bay. He loaded bags and passed them to where Dan and Kevin could shoulder them up the ladder and on deck, out into the skiff until the lights of Seattle had disappeared in the mists behind Whidby Island. He remembered how once Miss Emily had appeared with coffee and sandwiches, but this time the girl was up in the bows of her barnacle-encrusted namesake signaling with the lantern while the equally exhausted cook warped back skiffloads of coal to fire the *Fröya*'s insatiable boilers. Each time there was a moment's respite Dave would stretch out on a coal sack atop the bunkerful of cannel. Suddenly he came to with the realization that he had been asleep—that nobody had awakened him to shovel more coal.

Aching in every joint, he stared blearily about the bunker. His lantern had burned out, but daylight came from the open hatchway eighteen feet above. He struggled to his feet and tried not to think of what it must have been like for the boys to climb that ladder with a hundredweight of cannel on their backs. And the others: How must it have been to crawl about the *Fröya* stowing coal in every possible cranny and crevice, a hatful at a time, as they prepared for the Inside Passage? Dazedly, Dave realized that the tug was built for river traffic, for towing logs down the Duwamish, and not with sufficient bunkering for twelve days nonstop.

He made it to the deck and stood staggering for a moment. The *Fröya* was moving beneath a mushroom of black smoke, plowing majestically between pine-covered headlands less than a mile apart. On the left-hand shore rose smoke from what he supposed was a sawmill. The right bank seemed unchanged since the coming of the white man. He wondered if anyone lived there, then saw Indians paddling a serpent-headed dugout canoe. The Indians gave tug and tow an incurious glance and went back to tending their gill nets.

"Good morning, Mr. Watkins." It was the girl.

"Uh, yeah, uh, good morning." Dave forced himself the rest of the way into wakefulness. Even in a jersey and dungarees several sizes too large for her, this blond girl was unmistakably female. Dave considered the ordeal she had been through. "I'm sorry," he said.

"For what?"

"For not getting there sooner."

"Mr. Twofingers has been regaling me with your adventures. I'm sure you did your best."

"I hope I got there soon enough."

"Soon enough for what?"

Dave suddenly discovered he had at least one too many hands and feet. How, he wondered? What was the proper form for asking if a young lady had escaped a fate worse than death?

"Did they treat you bad in that uh—hotel?"

Miss Emily shrugged. "Apart from not being able to leave, it was no worse than any other time."

"Other time?" Dave managed.

"Why should it be?" the girl asked, her voice smooth and untroubled. "I always stay at the Hotel Yesler."

"You do?"

The girl stared. "It's a properly run establishment, sponsored by the YWCA."

It took Dave a moment to remember what YWCA stood for. He remembered the cable car gripman's odd look. So it really was a "ladies' hotel"! Dave didn't know whether to be happy or embarrassed. "Who was that woman did such a bang-up job of screamin'?"

The girl stared again. "I never knew her name. Some matron the detective agency sent to keep me from getting off to look for my father."

"Your father?"

"James Jerome, vice president of the North Valley Bank."

"I know who he is."

"But you don't know where he is, do you?"

"Last I knew he was conspirin' with the Okanogan County sheriff to steal my cattle—and the note wasn't even due yet!"

"Not my father, Mr. Watkins. Father went North seven months ago to raise funds. You see, when times stay bad for over four years, even banks can be hard pressed for cash." The girl worked a strand of hair out of her face and turned into the wind. "If anyone dealt less than honorably with you, it was most probably the same overanxious assistant who's been forcing unwelcome attentions on me—the same person I strongly suspect has been intercepting mail and causing me other inconveniences."

Dave stared. "Are you tellin' the truth this time, Miss Jerome? I been through a lot these last few days and I don't think I need any more lies."

"I'm sorry, Mr. Watkins. We've all been through a lot and I fear this is not the end of it. Had I known you better I might have confided in you from the beginning. I fear that inadvertently I may have increased your troubles."

"How?"

"Most probably the search for you would not have been

so diligent had Mr. Skanes not suspected I might be accompanying your party."

"Skanes! What's he got to do with it—with you?"

"Mr. Skanes came highly recommended by the central bank in Seattle. He's been in charge since Father went out seeking additional funds."

Dave sighed. "I'm sorry," he finally said.

"Sorry for what?"

"For not findin' a way to leave you somewhere safe in Seattle. Now you'll have to go all the way up to Skagway with us, and I don't know what luck you'll have catching a steamer back."

"But you don't understand, Mr. Watkins. Father went to Alaska. When I despaired of ever apprising him of the utter depravity of his substitute I was forced into extreme measures. But you're taking me to Alaska—exactly where I wish to go—oh, dear!"

"What's wrong?" Then Dave saw the skiff being let back from the stern of the *Fröya*. It was time to start coaling again.

During the next four days Dave managed to catch bits of rest between coalings. Now that the *Fröya* was bunkered against a blow, Twofingers and Taskoosh had transferred via the skiff back to the *Emily*, where they fed and watered cows, prodded those willing to lay down and die back onto their feet, and butcher one maverick for fresh meat, meanwhile winching half a dozen dead ones on deck and over the side. Aboard the *Fröya* Olsson and Ole spelled each other at the wheel while Whitefeather and the grocer who had provisioned them did their best to cook an occasional meal between firing boilers. After one disastrous attempt at ferrying a meal via the skiff, the *Emily*'s crew had settled for whatever Miss Emily could put together on the double-ovened coal burner of the square-rigger's twenty-year-dormant galley.

They were, by Crazy Mike's estimate, a little over half-way. "But you said twelve days if everything went right," Dave protested.

"Told ye I couldn't say till we got out in the open sea," the old man said. "Yer towhead skipper up there's doin' bet-ter'n I thought. Makin' about five and a half instead o' four."

"So we'll be there in another four days?"

"I didn't say that, boy. Look ahead."

Dave looked. "What's different?"

"Look again."

Dave had seen narrow passages of water between dark, pine-covered slopes nearly every time he had found a mo-ment to spare on deck. Occasionally there had been an hour at a time when no land was visible—usually on the left side, which he had by now learned to call port. At least two out of every three times he surfaced from his self-imposed night-mare of coal heaving, the fog had left only the vaguest hint of shore. He had expected to be seasick, but so far nobody had suffered from that malady, thanks to the sheltered waters of the Inland Passage.

Gradually he took in what was different about the sea this time. Long, steady seas were rolling in from port—west—where there was no island to break the force of the wind.

"Them waves got a fetch from here to Siberia," Crazy Mike cackled. "And we got close to a hundred miles with nowhere to run to."

"What do you mean?"

"Look up there."

Dave saw the mare's-tail clouds. It didn't take a seaman to know what that meant. He wondered why Olsson didn't run for shelter. But the shore east of them was bleak and rocky. The wind blew straight toward it. Dave stared at the *Fröya*. The tug was at an angle, and he thought at first that Olsson was turning for the shore. Then he realized it was just the wind that made the *Emily* tow askew off one quarter of the tug's low stern. While they watched, somebody on the tug began letting out the skiff for more coal.

It had not been paid out more than a hundred feet before Dave saw that the unladen skiff was blowing even farther alee than the *Emily*—so far that they would never be able to capture it. Whoever was paying out line on the *Fröya* saw it too. He began pulling the skiff back, but the tug was moving so crabwise against wind and current that suddenly the skiff was caught in a foaming maelstrom, just as the steam launch full of pirates had been caught five days ago. The bow dipped into the water. For an instant the skiff stood on end, then plummeted. A moment later it surfaced, but now Dave could see it was no longer keeping pace with them. The line had broken. Olsson was not about to waste time trying to recover it when they were this close to a lee shore. Dave wondered how they would transfer coal from now on. He wondered if it was the sudden rolling motion of the *Emily* that was making his stomach uneasy.

20

Two hours later there were no lingering doubts in Dave's mind. Dignity forgotten, he leaned over the lee rail to contribute a gastric offering to Poseidon. Beside him the boys were performing similar rites. Finally he wiped tears from his eyes and staggered below. The cattle were struggling to lay down, and once a cow went down in this crowded hold it would die.

Looking decidedly green despite their dark skin, Twofingers and Taskoosh struggled to keep gasping, heaving cows on their feet. Dave grabbed a pole and began prodding. Crazy Mike appeared, making Dave wonder momentarily how a decrepit peg leg could manage ladders when the *Emily* was rolling and heaving this way. "Give 'em salt," the old man said. "Plenty o' salt but no water till it stops blowing."

Dave was too sick himself to struggle for the reasoning behind this. He guessed the old man knew more about cattle boats than he. But how was he to do it? There were blocks of lick salt from the general store manager's defunct feed business, but his cows were too unhappy to lick at them. Dave struggled up on deck and across to the galley, where smoke blew fitfully from the Charlie Noble. Inside, Miss Emily seemed to be feeling the effects of this bumpy passage too, but the girl stuck gamely with her double-ovened stove, gasping and flapping a dish towel each time a stray gust sent smoke the wrong way down the Charlie Noble.

"Got any salt?" Dave asked.

The girl pointed.

"I mean a lot of it."

She had rigged a harness to keep herself and her chair from sliding back and forth across the splintered galley deck. She pointed again. Dave lurched across the low-ceilinged compartment and opened the pantry door. Pawing over sacks of flour, rice, beans, and sugar, he finally found what he needed. He got the gunny sack of table salt down below, and soon all five of the able-bodied men circulated among dying cattle, forcing mouths open, tossing a handful of salt as far down gaping throats as they could. The noise the cows made was different from any Dave had ever heard before. He suspected that if he survived this trip he would never be able to forget that sound.

Wind howled and whistled overhead, and occasionally a solid slug of seawater would come thundering down the hatch to add to the general confusion. Somewhere on deck Crazy Mike's peg leg was still sending cryptic telegrams as the old man stumped about. Finally Dave realized the captain was yelling at him. It seemed urgent. Dave looked up at the white-whiskered face that peered down the hatchway, and he had to climb halfway up before he could understand.

"Taking on too much water," the old man shrieked. "Git two more men up here and cover this hatch!"

Dave beckoned Taskoosh and Twofingers. After only twenty minutes of backbreaking, fingernail-tearing exertion, they had the hatch covered and were fitting canvas over it with nails and battens. Dave was ready to go down and tend cattle again when Crazy Mike got a mouth to his ear and made his voice heard above the moaning of the wind. "Two men to man the pump," he said. "Relief every twenty minutes."

Dave sighed and moved over to the job he had learned to

dread. Cows, being uninhibited with regard to sanitation, the hour spent each morning bowing to a man at the other end of the pump handle was endured amid the stench of the tawny liquid they pumped from the *Emily*'s hold. Dave caught a whiff of it even in this wind and promptly retched again.

He had learned by now that even the most desperate bout of seasickness could be alleviated by concentrating on something else. It was not an exercise in will, for in such contests the stomach will always come out ahead. But when a man is working physically at full capacity rowing, pumping, heaving on a halliard or sheet, there simply is no time to be sick. Doggedly, Dave manned the pump and even managed an encouraging grin for Taskoosh at the other end of the handle.

The *Emily* was moving with an agility not strictly in keeping for so elderly a lady, bow rising high above a swell, hovering poised for a heart-stopping moment before plunging downward with a corkscrewing motion to take the next sea like a foaming Niagara over the bow until the midships deck, where Dave and Taskoosh struggled with the pump, was momentarily waist deep in water.

They had grumbled days ago when Crazy Mike had insisted on making overworked men rig lifelines around the deck. Now Dave saw the wisdom of the peg-legged ancient's insistence. He was thinking about tying himself and Taskoosh to the pump when abruptly he felt it suck air and lose prime. The bilges were, for the time being, pumped dry.

He wondered how the boys were making out down below with the cattle. Smoke still gusted fitfully from the Charlie Noble, so he guessed Miss Emily's galley was functioning after a fashion. The *Fröya* wallowed at the end of the hawser, disappearing in low-scudding clouds half the time. Studying the tug, Dave finally realized that the hawser had been let out to twice its former length—to take up the shock and smooth the jerking between these curling seas, he supposed. He wondered if there was sufficient coal aboard to make it to some sheltered cove where they could anchor and come alongside for coaling again now that the skiff was gone.

It was, in spite of the alarming weather, the first time in days that Dave had had a moment alone to think. He wondered if Miss Emily was telling the truth this time. Or if she was telling the truth, was she telling all of it? It made sense in a weird sort of way. If Skanes was out to make a name for himself in the banking business, he would not be overly nice in his dealings with cattlemen whose notes were soon to fall due. And if that basso-voiced villain had taken a shine to Miss Emily it would explain the special zeal he had dedicated to making life miserable for the cattleman who, from his viewpoint, had supplanted Skanes in the girl's affections.

Dave wondered. He supposed that someday he would marry, such being the ordained scheme of things. But a hard-working cattleman in the Okanogan just didn't have that much time to go out courting, nor were there that many candidates for the dubious honor of being a wife on a cattle ranch in Conconully. He wondered what would happen if he were ever to hint at such a preposterous idea to a girl born in the lap of luxury, who talked proper English, a Jerome of the North Valley Bank Jeromes. Prudently, Dave decided it would be safest not to broach the subject. He had been laughed at and humiliated enough lately. Somewhere in Alaska he could deliver this unusual young lady to her father and get on with his own business.

His reverie was interrupted by a thin voice that barely carried over the wind. He turned and saw Crazy Mike up on the quarterdeck, protected somewhat by the whaleback wheelhouse. The old man was shouting into a megaphone and waving. Dave grasped the weather lifeline and made his way aft.

"Got to set the spanker," the old man said.

That was another new one on Dave. The old man pointed overhead until Dave understood that the spanker was the small, fore-and-aft sail on the rearmost mast. Gazing at the *Emily*'s high bow, which yawed this way and that with each plunge, Dave supposed that the small sail would serve as a weathercock to make the *Fröya*'s job easier.

Kevin Corcoran's broad, dark face appeared out of a scuttle, and Dave guessed that Crazy Mike had been shouting down a funnel too. The boy joined Dave on the quarterdeck, and after false starts and fumbles they had the canvas unlashed and were hauling away on throat and peak halliards. Dave wished repeatedly for an interpreter, wondering if Crazy Mike was being needlessly obscure or if seafaring men actually talked this way. Why, Dave wondered, was one rope called a halliard and another a sheet? Why did sheet refer to a rope and not to the canvas sail that that sheet braced into or out of the wind? Finally, the spanker had a second reef tied into it, peak and throat halliards drawn taut, and was sheeted amidships.

And even then Crazy Mike was not satisfied. As the wind rattled and flapped the canvas, first on one side and then the other, the *Emily* still yawed, though not so crazily as when she had been towed under bare poles. Under the old man's urging Dave slacked the starboard sheet while Kevin hauled in on the portside until the spanker was hauled around. Now it filled without flapping and the *Emily*'s bow headed slightly windward, easing the sideways pull on the towing hawser. It seemed to Dave's unaccustomed eyes that they were moving more easily now—perhaps even a fraction of a knot faster.

More importantly, as Crazy Mike explained over the wind, the square-rigger was no longer subjected to those head-snapping jerks as the towing hawser went alternately taut and slack. "'Nother hour o' that and ye'll part a hawser," the old man shrilled, "and then where'd ye be?"

Dave didn't know. He guessed he'd be just as happy if he

never found out. Thoughtfully, he went below to relieve somebody at prodding sick cows to their feet. The cattle were still moaning piteously, with a sound unlike anything he had ever heard on land. What, he wondered, would it be like to haul cattle on a really long run, like from the Argentine to Great Britain? Less than a week and Dave had firmly resolved that he would never sell another herd of these poor beasts to be butchered overseas—not if he could help it. There had to be a better way if a man in the cattle business still aspired to call himself a human being.

Above the sound of bawling cattle was another and more disquieting sound. It took Dave a moment to realize what it was; then he recognized the sloshing of full bilges. And they had pumped less than an hour ago! He tried to remember who had last had his chance at fresh air. Twofingers and young Dan were due. "You two on deck and man the pumps," he said. "And make sure you tie yourselves down good." The Indians nodded and began struggling up the ladder. Dave picked up a pole and began tormenting a dying cow back onto its feet.

Somewhere in another bay of this hold he could hear Arnold Taskoosh urging cows to open their fool mouths and have a little salt. The Indians had all been cheerful and uncomplaining despite hardship and uncertainty far from home. It worried Dave. They were his people and his responsibility. If they had complained or shirked he could have taken it in stride, but . . . they had worked so hard for so little. He had to get this herd through somehow—get some cash money for a change and make it up to them. He thought wistful, goatish thoughts of the quietly competent Miss Emily, who did everything well—from riding to sailing to cooking to—lying. Such calm confidence could come only from the innate knowledge that she was a Jerome, that no matter what went wrong there was the family name and the family money. Jeromes never really suffered—never missed more than one meal at a time. He had to be out of his mind if he thought the lissome blonde in jersey and dungarees would even think of spending a winter in Conconully.

They were almost halfway to Skagway. He had pumped the peg-legged skipper about Alaska, and Crazy Mike had favored him with a half year's accumulation of the Seattle *Star*. The story of the new strike in the Klondike was well documented. It was true. There was gold there; there were hungry men up there, and in September of last year, in eighteen and ninety-six, beef had sold in Circle City for forty-eight dollars. Not forty-eight dollars a cow, which was triple the Seattle price, if they were buying. Dave had read and reread the article in the Seattle *Star*. There was no way around it. In Circle City beef had sold for *forty-eight dollars a pound!* But there was another side to the coin. Circle City was five hundred miles measured by air from Skagway. Dawson, where the last strike was reported, was three hundred fifty—and considerably farther, he supposed, if one followed the series of rivers, lakes, and swamps that constituted the trail.

Nor was it to be an easy initiation, according to the published reports. To get to the Klondike one had to go through either White Pass or Chilkoot. The latter was not properly a road. It was a rather steep staircase hacked out of the mountainside. Men packed their supplies up over the Chilkoot crowded so close on each other's heels that each man had to wait for the man ahead of him to take one step at a time. The local Indians were small Tlingits with scanty mustaches who looked much more oriental than Dave's people. The Tlingits had learned the value of money, and each day they raised their rates for packing goods over the Chilkoot. For a herd of cattle . . .

White Pass was only slightly better. When it was not frozen solid it was a bog. This time of year it was anybody's guess which he would find—mud or ice. Either way there would be no grass for a herd—they were shipping in hay and shorts for packhorses from Seattle! He considered the

Chilkat and Dalton trail, where some enterprising capitalist had put in a telpherage system to haul supplies to the summit of the pass with ropes and pulleys. Chilkoot, Chilkat, White—none of these passes would let a cow through alive. And these were only the beginning of the hundreds of miles through barren territory where snow fell regularly in September, where during a brief summer the temperature could climb to ninety—and plummet in winter to seventy-five below!

He had considered Valdez instead of Skagway for a beginning—Valdez, where it had been four below zero last April Fool's Day. But Valdez was three hundred unprotected miles west of Skagway across the treacherous Gulf of Alaska. If they were already having problems and not three hours into the open sea north of Prince Rupert . . . why, Dave wondered, had he ever considered this crazy idea? He should have stayed in Seattle and taken his chances—maybe headed back home, like the red-headed puncher he had met coming down out of the mountains.

"Hey, Dave!" It was Hodge Twofingers, who belonged on deck manning the bilge pump. "Dave, you better come up here. We got big trouble!"

21

We're sinking, Dave decided. But above the bawl-moaning of suffering cows he had been keeping one ear cocked for the sound of sloshing bilge water. Slowly Twofingers and young Sinlahekin had been getting it under control. He put down his prod and climbed wearily up the ladder.

On deck the wind was unchanged, still shrieking dismally over the *Emily* from the bow. Then he sensed that it had changed. Either the *Emily* was on a different heading or the wind had shifted. He glanced aft and the spanker was backing, filling from the wrong side. He was heading aft when he heard the commotion up in the bows. Two of his Indians struggled to coil the hawser that the other two were winching in with the capstan. Dave stared, amazed. How could only two men walking around those capstan bars manage to pull the *Emily* closer to the tug against this wind? And why should they want to?

He trotted forward, keeping a weather eye on the seas and the lifelines. He put his weight to one of the capstan bars, and the hawser began coming in a little faster. As he circled close to the bow on his trip around the capstan he saw that the hawser was not taut any more. It lay slack in the water. He squinted into the scud of horizontally moving spray and rain. "Where's the *Fröya?*" he demanded.

The others shrugged and kept on winching. Five minutes passed while Dave worked up a sweat in spite of the near-freezing spray, and then his question was answered after a fashion. He didn't know where the tug was, but as the frayed end of the six-inch manila hawser trailed dripping through the eye, Dave abruptly knew where the tug was not. The *Emily* was adrift and alone. He wondered how many miles they were off that rocky coast.

He was running aft to where Crazy Mike waved and shouted unintelligibly from the whaleback wheelhouse when Miss Emily opened the door of the galley. "Mr. Watkins," she called, "the others have eaten. Whenever you're ready—"

"Later—" he managed, passing her by at a dead gallop. Halfway down the low midships deck a wave caught him. He grabbed for the lifeline, missed, and was swept across the deck. Barely in time, he caught the lee line and saved himself from immediate death. He wondered if he'd made a mistake.

"You got any ideas, old man?" he demanded of Crazy Mike.

"Aye. But I'll need a revolver."

Dave stared. "What for?"

"How else you get men to go aloft on a night like this?"

Dave didn't know. He considered this old man's experience with shanghaied crews—drunkards, misfits, jailbirds. He wondered if ever there had been a day when honest men went to sea, did an honest day's work, and were treated with the respect an honest job deserved. Still staring at the white-whiskered wreck, he finally asked, "Have you ever tried explaining why it has to be done?"

From the old man's look of surprise Dave knew this was one thought that had never occurred to him. "Now what do we have to do?" Dave asked.

Crazy Mike pointed aloft at a forest of masts and spars that tilted and gyrated crazily with each roll of the *Emily's* barnacle-fouled hull. "If I had a crew knew what they's doin' I'd set the lower tops'ls on second reef; but even on a fair-weather climb you lubbers 'd foul it up." He hesitated and did a little dance of impatience on his peg leg. "We got maybe ten miles of sea room. Stand around here jawin' and we're all dead in one hour. Git yer savages up there and set all the stays'ls and the last two jibs an' maybe we can claw off."

"You mean we can actually sail away into the wind?"

"We could of twenty years ago. Still could if poor old *Emily*'d been anchored twenty-four hours in fresh water, then dry-docked and scraped."

Dave studied the reeling forest of masts. "If we can't do it, then why do my people have to climb up there?"

"'Cause if you don't do it you're dead in one hour. Do it and ye may hold us off. Poor old *Emily*'s too foul to make a long board into the wind, but maybe we can keep from goin' back'ards."

Dave studied the mass of stays that ran fore and aft between the masts. He studied the motion of the *Emily* and of the sea. He considered Crazy Mike's one-hour alternative. It was a compelling reason. He went forward to explain it to his people. Before he had properly begun, Dave was confused.

"I ain't no sailor," he conceded. "Let's go aft and get him to tell us how to do it."

"Mutiny, by God!" Crazy Mike raged as they trotted en masse onto the quarterdeck.

Dave made reference to an inedible by-product of the male cow. "Now say it simple," he demanded. "Tell each man what he's got to do."

Crazy Mike stared unbelieving for a moment. He swallowed a couple of times and then began to explain.

For Dave his first climb aloft was undiluted horror. Ten times he wished he dared go back down and compose himself for death on a rocky coast. The only thing that kept him from turning totally chicken was Taskoosh and Twofingers blithely climbing above and below him.

Resting on the tiny platform around the lubber hole, he saw Dan and Kevin climbing the next mast to the rear with equal unconcern. He remembered hearing somewhere that Indians seemed totally unafraid of heights. Now he could believe it. Finally they were in position, struggling with salt-stiffened knots. The triangular stays'ls popped like cannons as they were freed of lashings, threatening to flap themselves to pieces before Dan and Twofingers could scramble down on deck again to sheet in.

As the stays'ls filled, the *Emily's* frantic corkscrewing became less vigorous. She lay over alee, still rising with each swell, but no longer rolling now that she had some canvas to steady her. Dave gazed straight down into foaming water. To his surprise it was moving backward. They were making way!

He struggled to remember Crazy Mike's instructions and unlash the next stays'l in proper sequence. Another cannon pop, another colossally thunderous flapping, and then the *Emily* lay over even farther as the men on deck sheeted her in. The lee rail was under water now. Dave wondered how his cattle were taking it. Maybe better, he hoped, for in spite of the decks being canted, their angle was fairly constant. It was better than the uncontrolled rolling under tow.

He glanced astern where Crazy Mike struggled feebly with the stiff steering gear. The old man was gesturing again, beckoning them to come down. "We got 'nother one to do yet," Taskoosh protested.

Dave pointed at green water surging over the lee rail. "I think we got enough canvas on her for now."

Going back down was even harder for Dave than climbing up. He marveled at the unconcerned way the Indians went down the shrouds, as casually as if they were strolling Conconully's single street. Finally he closed his eyes and felt his way down one careful foot and handhold at a time. It seemed easier that way. Once on deck he knew he would faint if he didn't keep moving. Hands on the lifeline, he made it aft to the quarterdeck. "Hold 'er nor'west by north," Crazy Mike shouted, and let go of the wheel.

"Hold it!" Dave yelled. "Wait a goddamn minute. What's norris, and how do I—"

The old man spun on his peg leg and struggled with the wheel again. "See that point on the lubber line?" There was a moment of confusion while Dave learned what a lubber line was, then got it straight in his head which point on the compass rose was to be kept on this line. The first time he turned the wheel the compass swung in the wrong direction. There were sudden flapping noises, and Crazy Mike shrieked and chittered to strange gods as he struggled feebly to keep the *Emily* from going in stays.

Once Dave saw which way the old man wanted to turn the wheel, he helped. After a couple of minutes' supervision the skipper dared leave him alone at the wheel. "Tired," he managed. "Got to git some coffee."

An hour later Dave was still alone in the whaleback wheelhouse, his back sheltered from the spray as he struggled to keep the proper petal of the compass rose swinging beneath the lubber line. The tiny binnacle lamp flickered occasionally and he wondered what he would do if it were to go out.

He could, he guessed, steer by the feel of the wind on his face. After a while he began to get the feel of the ship, learning to point high into the wind whenever it gusted, hoping thus to compensate for the times when sails fluttered and flapped, forcing him to sail alee of their compass heading unless he wished to lose steerageway. The wind, as near as he could tell, blew steadily from the same direction. He wondered how long the storm would last. He wondered where he was—if any land lay ahead. The night was impenetrable, and his eyes, focused on the dimly lit compass card in the binnacle, could see nothing else. What time of night was it? Would Crazy Mike ever come back? Each time he thought the wind was abating it gusted again, driving the *Emily's* lee rail under. The old lady was moving, but he remembered the peg-legged skipper's warning.

Not even power boats moved in straight lines, he had learned from days of studying the *Fröya's* crabbed angle at the other end of the hawser. If the *Emily* had a bottom freshly scraped and painted she might not wallow quite so disconsolately leeward. He wondered if they were making any progress windward at all—or was all this frantic activity merely postponing an inevitable rendezvous with the rocky shore east of here?

Somewhere out there in all that fog and spray and confused seas the *Fröya* would be casting back and forth, trying to find them. But if Dave couldn't see halfway to the *Emily's* bow, what chances were there of the *Fröya* ever finding them? He endured another eternity, steering automatically, his eyes and his whole being fixed on the relationship between the lubber line and the next petal clockwise from the red "NW" on the compass card.

Abruptly a face appeared at his feet. Dave was startled, then saw it was Twofingers climbing the ladder up onto the quarterdeck. "Miss Emily says you go eat," the Indian said.

"Where the hell's Crazy Mike?"

"Fell asleep in the galley. He looks kind of bad."

"He always looks bad."

"I know," Twofingers shouted back, "but he ain't slept for a couple of days. This time I think maybe the old man dies."

My cup runneth over, Dave thought. He would die soon himself if he didn't get some food and coffee into his empty midsection. He spent several minutes explaining to Twofingers how to steer, waited while Twofingers made the same mistake he made of turning the wheel in the logical direction only to see the compass card spin crazily the other way. Finally he guessed the Indian had gotten it through his head. "I'll be back as soon as I can," he promised and went below.

The lifelines were still necessary to get across the midships section, but now that the *Emily* was under sail she was not quite so awash. He made it to the galley without major disaster.

"Well, Mr. Watkins," Emily greeted, "do you think we'll survive?"

Dave wasn't sure. From the girl's sudden consternation he guessed everybody else must have been lying to cheer her up. "How's the old man?" he asked.

She pointed. Crazy Mike lay propped in a corner, a couple of chairs wedged against the settee so he wouldn't fall out. Asleep, he seemed even more decrepit, more defenseless than before. But the pallid, white-haired wreck was breathing steadily. Dave guessed he'd better leave him alone.

Miss Emily tapped his shoulder. Even after struggling for hours in this blow with pots wedged into the fiddley atop the coal-burning Shipmate, her blond head that close to Dave's was disquieting. She pointed at a table where she had wedged a cup of coffee and a bowl of burgoo for him. Until Dave got the first mouthful of the stew down he didn't realize how empty his seasick digestive system had become.

The girl waited till he had finished eating. "More?" she asked. Dave was tempted but he didn't want to lose what he had already. Better stay hungry, he guessed. He was getting to his feet on the sloping galley deck when she asked, "Mr. Watkins, do you know where we are?"

"Within a hundred yards," he said, and exited the galley. Feeling his way aft along the lifeline, he reflected that he wasn't exactly lying. He knew exactly where the *Emily* was. The only thing he didn't know was where everything else on earth was. From the feel of the ship he guessed Twofingers had committed no gross errors in steering. He felt his way along the aft bulkhead and found Crazy Mike's cabin.

The dirty-old-man-alone smell was so overpowering that he left the door on the hook despite the icy wind. Trying to remember where Twofingers had found the matches the night they had surprised the old man at the coaling dock, he scrabbled around bumping into things until finally he had the gimbaled case-oil lamp aglow.

The wind rattled charts until he had to give up and close the door. Finally he managed to spread out a tattered and much-scribbled-on sheet of heavy paper and struggled to make some sense out of the old man's crabbed notation.

There was a snaky line with dates and hours scribbled beside it. Dave didn't know the date, nor did he know the hour. Then he heard the brass chronometer on the bulkhead strike. Three bells, according to Dave's landlocked horological sense, did not agree with one-thirty. He supposed he'd better believe what the hands on the clock said. If that was so, then the old man had positioned the *Emily* west of Prince Rupert some five hours ago. Sailing on a WNW heading . . . Dave suspected there were things like magnetic deviation to consider. There were currents. There was drift.

He wondered if Crazy Mike had been intending to head out due west into the open sea. It made sense, he supposed, to get as far away from land as possible. But how would they ever find the *Fröya* again? Poring over the chart, he tried to guess which way this combination of wind and drift and an unknown magnetic deviation would actually take him. If he was thinking right they ought to be making a true course barely west of north.

The wind was growing fitful now, gusting and then dying for seconds at a time. He supposed Twofingers had his hands full trying to hold a heading. Was the storm ending? Then, once more studying the chart before him, Dave knew what that fitful wind had to mean. They had sailed into the lee of Dundas Island.

He went on deck. It was still impossible to see the length

of the *Emily*, but from the sudden calm he knew there had to be something out there windward to stop the force of the waves.

So now what? The *Emily* would no longer respond to the helm. He studied the cryptic numbers that dotted the water east of Dundas Island on the chart, hoping they meant what he thought they did. There was a lee shore less than ten miles east of here. Another few miles north was land. South lay the open sea and those crippling coamers. He went back forward to the galley and found Twofingers dozing in a corner. "Get everybody up on deck," he said.

"Wha' happen? Something wrong?"

"I hope not," Dave said. "We're going to take in sail and drop anchor."

22

It was still blowing a day later when the *Fröya* came alongside. "Hello, stranger, you got maybe some coal you could spare?" Olsson shouted.

In the faint hope that something like this might happen, Dave had put his people to piling several tons of cannel on the midships deck. The *Fröya* put out fenders and tied alongside. They began tossing coal down onto the tug. Dave could see the bleak shore of Dundas Island now. At least he thought it was Dundas Island, for since he had fallen asleep, Crazy Mike had not yet seemed to come fully awake. Dave wondered if it was just old age or if the poor old man had overexerted himself, possibly for the last time in a long, strenuous life.

"You're lucky," Olsson said over coffee.

"I know," Dave said. "How'd you find me?"

"It had to be here or nowhere," the tug skipper said. "But you don't never want to anchor. What happen to you if the wind shift?"

"What should I have done?"

"Heave to—maybe just sail back and forth."

Which would be fine, Dave guessed, if he knew how. John Whitefeather appeared, his lined face darker than usual and his braids no longer shiny, thanks to days of heaving coal. Dave found a moment to wonder what his pale face must look like. "Bad?" the older man asked.

Dave shrugged. "We're alive."

"How's the feed holdin' out?"

"Fine," Dave said. Which was true. The cattle had not eaten nearly what he had expected. Seasick cows, he guessed, were just not that hungry. What he did not mention to Whitefeather was his growing worry over water.

"About that hawser—" he turned to Olsson.

"Maybe you get by wit'out that trouble if the old man set the spanker sooner," the tugboat skipper ventured.

"Will it happen again?"

Olsson threw up his hands. "Ve got maybe five, six days yet to Skagway. How the hell I know what's gonna happen?"

"But it's mostly sheltered from here on, isn't it?"

"Mostly. Maybe we be lucky and get no more trouble."

But it was seven more days, thanks to fogs and having to wait hours at a time for tidal rips to reverse before the *Fröya* dared try to shoot the Wrangell Narrows and, three days later, another tricky passage where a reviving Crazy Mike assured him that up on the hillside behind that fog lay Juneau. Then finally, down to the last sip of water and coal, tug and tow progressed beneath a stately fountain of smoke and sparks up the final eighty miles of the Lynn Canal, sides so straight, so vertical, and so parallel that it was hard to believe it had not been dug by some crazy Frenchman as a preliminary for the one to come in Panama.

The Lynn Canal was crowded with every conceivable kind of shipping, from oceangoing liners and freighters to dugout canoes paddled by impassive Tlingits. Tugs towed scows, some with tents erected on the flat and totally exposed decks of these scows. Dave stared unbelieving. Had men traveled all the way from Seattle like this?

But if he was amazed by the variety of shipping that coursed up and down the busy Lynn Canal on the way to Skagway—that town was as unbelievable as a branch office of hell. Tents, false-fronted buildings, one rickety dock that seemed to have been completed only days ago; men too impatient or impoverished to use the dock pushed off from the beach with every conceivable size and shape of boat, raft, or float to lighter in supplies from the ships that lay crowded at anchor in the narrow roadstead.

On shore men bustled like ants, bearing loads twice their size as they slogged up through the interminable mudflats of this tidal bore to deposit precious supplies above the high-water mark where the mud was only knee deep. Behind the town a trail led up to the tent city of Dyea, where gold-seekers paused for their last taste of civilization in a single tent-saloon before facing the horror of another climb up the ice stairs of the Chilkoot, locked into an immovable human chain as each man waited for the man above him to take one more step.

In Skagway too waited the men on their way back from the Klondike, scattering gold dust like snuff, struggling to toss away a fortune as they whiled away the wait for the next steamer South. As the *Fröya* winched in hawser and cut loose to edge around behind and nudge the *Emily* between a scow and a hastily converted river steamer that had somehow survived the Inside Passage, Dave heard shooting.

During the hour it took to get anchors out bow and stern to keep the *Emily* from swinging in the confined space, he learned that there was always shooting in Skagway, always somebody getting killed, and that usually nobody paid much attention. He studied the single dock. There was no way on God's earth that he was ever going to lighter cows ashore through that mud. It was as bad as the Duwamish.

A short, heavy-shouldered Tlingit with a mandarin mustache appeared beside the *Emily* in a dugout. "You wan' go shore?" he called. "Two dollah."

Dave had been warned. But *two dollars!* Without thinking he blurted, "*Ip dolla*" in the language his Indians spoke down in Conconully.

"Heylo!" The Tlingit shook his head, then from the corner of his eye saw another dugout approaching. *"Dollah p'sit-cum,"* he compromised.

Dave was resigned to paying a dollar and a half when Whitefeather plucked his arm. "Only little bit water left," the older man said. "Give it all to them so they look nice and fat, or . . . ?"

"Go for broke," Dave said. If he didn't get feed and water into those cows soon there would be nothing to sell. He turned back to the rail and the dugout was gone. Clad once more in her dressing gown, which had been pinned and stitched into a semblance of respectability—with a seaman's jersey over the low neckline—Miss Emily was also gone.

Dave sighed. Later, when his immediate worries were over—once he had managed to transmute this herd into some of that imperishable yellow metal that everyone tossed around on shore—someday there would be time to grieve and maunder over what might have been. He supposed it was better this way. Any good-bye would be awkward. What could they say to each other? It was, he supposed, his last surprise from this unpredictable young lady.

A skiff bumped the side of the *Emily*. Dave looked down and saw a pepper-and-salt-suited man in a derby clambering up the boarding ladder. "Whatcha got?" the stranger asked.

"Fresh beef."

"On the hoof?"

"There's some other way to keep it fresh?" Dave wondered.

"How many?"

"Somewhere between six and eight hundred," Dave guessed.

"Eighty dollars," the stranger said briskly, "delivered on the beach."

"Been nice talkin' to you," Dave said.

"No need to get huffy. Ninety."

"You own the dock?"

"If I did, do you think I'd be out here?"

"How much a head's it goin' to cost to git these critters unloaded?"

"I'll give you fifty a head and unload them myself."

Which gave Dave a fair idea of what it was going to cost him to get his cows offloaded. Forty dollars a head!

Another bump against the side of the *Emily*. This time a mandarin-mustached Tlingit had paddled out a heavy man in muttonchop whiskers and blue serge. "Ah, cows, is it?" Which proved either that he was more observant or the williwaw wind had shifted again. Squinting at the first stranger he asked, "What'd he offer you?"

Dave was suspecting he was going to enjoy doing business in Skagway when young Kevin stuck his head up out of the hatch. "Hey, Dave, you want to give them all the—"

"Give 'em all they want to eat!" Dave roared. If these buyers were to learn how fine he was cutting it with feed and water . . . He added a brief instruction in the old language for Kevin and all the others to get below, stay below, and keep their mouths shut for a while. From the corner of his eye he saw the Tlingit in the dugout studying him thoughtfully. He wondered how close their languages were. Could the impassive Indian with the mandarin mustache understand everything he was saying?

"A hundred and I'll get 'em ashore," the first stranger offered.

Visions of sugarplums danced through Dave's head. Even after he'd paid off the bank, the skipper of the *Evalina*, paid off Olsson, and made some kind of arrangement with Crazy Mike, it would still be more money than he had ever dreamed of owning. With that kind of money he might even think about a new house on the ranch and a new wife to . . . Abruptly he didn't want to think about that.

The pepper-and-salt-suited stranger misread Dave's distress. "A hundred and ten!"

Dave sighed and faced the pair. "I keep hopin' I'll run

into an honest man someday," he grumbled. "Now, you know what beef's sellin' for in that town. More likely, you know what it would sell for if any of those bean-eatin' millionaires could get their jaws around a hunk of it. And if you come from the States you know how much it cost me to git it up here. Now let's see if you can come up with a real offer." He hesitated a moment before adding, "And don't try to tell some pore old cowhand this ain't the first live beef you've seen in months—not until you learn how to play poker with Indians."

A third boat bumped the side of the *Emily,* and before Dave had time to look he heard a familiar voice saying, "One dollar and that's final. Now go get yourself a cutlass if you wish to play pirate." A moment later Miss Emily's blond head appeared. "Don't believe anything they tell you, Mr. Watkins," she called. "I've an offer for your beef. *Oh!*" Abruptly she stopped, staring at the man in blue serge and muttonchops who, Dave realized, had yet to make his first offer.

The girl recovered immediately. Dave wondered if one of Skanes' men had managed to beat them up here. The man with the muttonchop whiskers stared from Dave to the girl, then back at Dave. "Umm," he ummed. "From Conconully, aren't you?" He pointed at the stack of hides salvaged from dead cows. "Know the brand," he explained. "Knew your father too. Give you a hundred eighty a head."

"Father, that's outrageous and you know it!" the girl blazed. "Mr. Watkins has saved my life on numerous occasions. He has transported me to Skagway. In addition, Mr. Watkins honors you by seeking my hand. You'll pay him two hundred thirty a head—two hundred in gold and the remainder in negotiable paper."

Dave's look of full and complete discombooberation was not lost on James Jerome, vice president of the North Valley Bank, and father of the blond, twenty-four-year-old and no-visible-defects young lady in pinned-together peignoir and   G 2 seaman's jersey. He gave Dave a look of amused commiseration. "You'll learn to live with it," the older man muttered.

Later that afternoon, when the *Emily* had been nudged into the dock and the *Fröya* lay alongside with Ole manning the winch that hoisted bawling cows up onto the dock for their first fresh air in nearly two weeks, Dave was still floating bemusedly when the girl appeared beside him. Handing him coffee and a sandwich, she said, "Of course I won't hold you to that part of the deal, Mr. Watkins. It's just that Father always thinks of the bank first, and I find the best way of bargaining is to keep the other party always slightly off balance."

"Oh?" Dave managed. He tried to remember his own advice about playing poker with Indians, but the girl gave him a shrewd look and he knew he was not fooling her. Her look softened.

"Of course, Mr. Watkins," she continued in a changed tone, "if you are amenable, please be assured the offer was made in good faith."

Dave rounded on her. "Goldang it!" he snarled. "Can't you ever talk plain?"

"Any time, Mr. Watkins."

Which put Dave in a position where he had no choice but to go on with this infuriating conversation. He wondered what it was going to be like to live with a wife who was always one jump ahead. As Mr. Jerome had suggested, maybe he would learn to live with it. Maybe even learn to like it, he guessed.

"Hey, Dave!" It was John Whitefeather sticking his head up out of the hatch. Then the old Indian saw what Dave and Miss Emily were doing. He gave a quiet smile and ducked back down the hatch.